MANTIS FORCE

MARIUM KAHNET

DECIMATION

A novel by

R. J. Amezcua

ISBN: 978-0-9980748-4-9 (pbk.)
ISBN: 978-0-9980748-5-6 (Ebk.)

QUENTOREX
S T U D I O S

www.mariumkahnet.com

www.mantisforce.com

info@quentorexstudios.com

To

MY WIFE

SHERYL

who blessed me with her editing skills

for my first book trilogy

and to whom

this book

is

Lovingly Dedicated

CONTENTS

Chapter One

LETALIS

The grey-blue Letalis moon's luminescence made the natural beauty of the undisturbed snow blanketing the grounds of the Stadageo glisten like sparkling diamonds. In stark contrast to the serenity of the surface, the noisy hive of activity of both humanoid and machinery operations echoed loudly throughout the subterranean superstructure, as they hastily prepared for the official transition of ownership of the Stadageo to the Letalis government. Nia Xongol and her sister-in-law Taona Xongol, acting on the message they had received from their fellow rogue sisters the day before yesterday, timed their mission of revenge accordingly.

After completing a long work shift, as they had done numerous times before, they passed through the last security checkpoint. The years of planning for this day, and the months of putting all the pieces in motion, had been long and arduous, often more dangerous than either had ever anticipated. But today was the end.

Nia and Taona made haste toward the transportation hub used exclusively for those who worked deep within the complex. Under the controlled surface of their demeanor, adrenaline flooded their bodies, and the urge to run thrummed in their blood stream to the rhythm of their swiftly beating hearts. They were hoping with every step and every breath that the built-in safety mechanisms they'd disabled would hold, and that the explosives strategically placed around the complex would not be found before they detonated.

Their answer would come in just a few short moments, after the cascade of uncontrolled power surges ultimately led to catastrophic failures of the auxiliary power cores, culminating in the utter destruction of the Stadageo's primary pod infrastructure.

Focused on keeping their actions normal, they gave small nods of acknowledgement to a cluster of Guyyian engineers exiting one of the smaller transportation shuttles. The nocturnal Guyyians seemed to become more energized during the fourth watch of the night.

Nia shivered a bit, noticing Taona's gaze tracking the bright lights of the transports carrying workers home. "Come on!" Nia said impatiently, in an undertone too soft for any nearby listening devices to pick up.

They entered a small shuttle and held their breath for a moment, for the pungent odor of the previous alien passengers lingered in the air. Taona hurried to properly enter the authorization codes to leave the transportation hub.

"Time to go home, my friend." Taona's calm melodic voice held a note of empathy as she powered up the shuttle's main power core. It brought a sense of normalcy to the moment.

Nodding sadly, Nia held back a rush of emotion that unexpectedly threatened to surface. *Why have I been so tormented with this unfathomable depth of sorrow lately? Be strong, capture and subdue your emotions.* Her lips firmed as she dwelt on those words. "Yes, let's go home," Nia said flatly.

Lifting off, they hardened their hearts, noticing a large transportation shuttle expelling workers—a shuttle that, they knew, would not be carrying many of those workers back home. Nia's growing sense of guilt at the unavoidable fallout of the coming destruction would hopefully vanish just like their ship as it entered bilious black storm clouds. A grim quiet descended upon them, and Taona removed a tiny device from the heel of her work boot, placing it on the shuttle's main control panel. Pressing the top section, the device immediately activated and lit up bright green just a couple short moments later. A gusty sigh of relief slipped out of Taona as she said, "No hidden or encrypted transmission links detected."

"That makes me happy, but I am sure the shuttle will be scanned eventually." Nia's somber tone was not lost on her dear friend.

"Look, I will leave it on just in case that happens." Taona grinned at Nia encouragingly.

Nia, trapped in worry, ignored the reassuring gesture and focused on adjusting the shuttle's speed to match the pace of other ships headed in the same direction. Something was niggling in the back of her mind and her spirit was greatly disturbed.

"Do you sense something wrong, besides the obvious?" Taona's question paralleled Nia's troubling thoughts.

Nia stared into Taona's Cymbratar-mutated, blue-speckled brown eyes, and a long pause ensued as she struggled to wrap her mind around the question. "I am not sure, but I think we overlooked something important," Nia said.

"Nia, I think you are right, that resonates strongly in my spirit," Taona said quietly. "What did we miss?" She continued keeping her tone carefully emotionless, and activated the ship's auto pilot function.

Nia closed her eyes, leaned back in her chair, and gazed intently into her mind's eye, rehearsing their previous actions, examining the mission down to the minutest detail. "I don't see…" Her hand flew to her mouth mid-sentence and she looked at Taona in wide-eyed shock as the answer came suddenly.

"Cremindraux Radiation Residue Containment Modules!" they spoke in unison. Their sole attention had been on smuggling the necessary explosive devices, planning escape routes, and completing the mission to destroy the Stadageo's primary stasis infrastructure. They had overlooked the potential of a major multiphasic radiation catastrophe that would kill an untold number of innocent civilians.

"We cannot go back." Nia's voice broke with impending tears. "The explosives will be detonating by now," she cried through hands cupped over her face. "What have we done?" Her voice turned to a harsh whisper as she bent forward, folding her torso to her thighs.

"Let us pray that any radiation leaks will be sealed under hundreds of meters of Stadageo rubble," Taona said softly, in perfect sympathy.

"I wonder if our prayers will even be heard." Nia's voice was fraught with the hopelessness she felt. Searching for relief, she reached into her winter uniform and retrieved the remainder of a protein wafer, as if it would soothe the burgeoning pain in her spirit. Her lip curled in revulsion as she realized the pitiful boon could not bring relief. "Would you like the rest of this?" She offered the packet to Taona.

"No, I have lost my appetite." Taona's index finger shot to her lips in a hushing motion. She pointed at the small detection device on the main flight control panel, which had just turned red, indicating that their ship's internal systems and logs were being checked by Stadageo security.

"The detonations must have just happened," Taona said in a murmur. Her body was tense. "They will probably do a follow up communication after the system checks are complete."

In an instant, the entire control panel lit up with flashing lights and loud alarms. Both women gripped the armrests of their seats as the shuttle was buffeted by a strong energy pulse wave. "Energy overload." Taona grunted as she plucked the smoking detection device from the control panel, blowing strongly on it to cool it down. She slid it into her vest pocket.

"Mission accomplished. It seems we were a little too concerned about..." Nia stopped speaking as they were violently thrown back into their seats. The shuttle had been hit by a much larger, intense energy wave.

The shrieks and screeches of overloaded systems filled the cockpit, and large sections of the control panel blacked out as they went offline. "We have lost part of the main power core!" Nia shouted in a panic, as the ship began to plummet nearly out of control. She shot out of her seat and rushed to the shuttle's main power distribution compartment to find and fix the problem.

"Activating Emergency Landing Sequence," Taona yelled.

Nia, an expert in a multitude of propulsion systems, quickly restarted the ship's main power core. "I got it!"

Their bodies felt gravity shift back to normal as the shuttle pulled up from its nosedive. Taona loosened her tense grip on the manual controls and steadied the ship, disengaging the ELC with a sigh.

"Most of the navigation systems are damaged," Nia said, bracing her hand on Taona's shoulder as she resettled herself into the adjoining pilot seat. "The power core oscillators were hit the hardest, and my temporary fix won't last very long." She shook her head. "Looks like our worst fears just happened."

Taona glanced briefly at Nia's set expression. "Maybe, but we don't know for sure Nia, so don't worry about it." A quiet descended around them as they emerged from the storm clouds. In the distance, the bright twinkling of the stars outlined the silhouette of the City of Perrapenta, now cloaked in utter darkness.

"Looks like the city's entire power grid system is offline," Nia commented as she reduced the shuttle's speed. "Do you see something missing?" She looked at Taona, whose brows rose questioningly.

"No ship traffic..." Taona's words trailed off as she came to the same conclusion.

"No ship traffic," Nia grimly repeated. "Civilian ships do not have multiphasic shielding like Stadageo work shuttles."

Taona took in a large breath, then released the built up anxiety in a huff. "Hundreds of ships must have crashed-landed," she said bluntly.

"More like thousands," Nia retorted bitterly. "But moreover, it will look suspicious for us to return to assist at the Stadageo."

"Nia, we knew this might happen." Taona disengaged the forward thrusters, hovering the ship over a frozen lake, then continued, "Perrapenta's power systems are down. It would be suicide if we tried to land there. We would be flying blind. Besides, our very presence would bring us to the attention of the authorities."

"I suppose you're right. Our families will be fine once the main power is back online." Nia inhaled a deep breath. "I guess going home is now out of the question." Her voice wavered a little with regret. She sniffed solidly, and then with resolve set thoughts of her grown adopted children aside.

"Well, we've been over this before." Taona's voice was laced with some impatience. "So, we need to get to the nearest city and use our family ties to the Muak'Xod to get what we need. This ship is too damaged to make our escape back to Ramah. We will need to get another one."

"I know this is one of our contingencies, do you remember?" Nia said softly with some pain in her tone. "I trust my husband to a certain extent, but I have also seen how brutally he has dealt with those who cross him. And another concern I have is, who knows who will take notice of us when we should be reporting to the Overseers? So let's do it as quickly as possible then," Nia said decisively with veiled eyes. She had only shared some of the challenges she had faced at home with Taona.

"You're right, let's go." Taona used her gloved hands to clear the burnt residue off of the control panel as best she could. "Looks like the auto-navigation functions are offline. So, I think it's best if you fly the ship manually, Nia."

"No way! You have a lot more experience flying these types of shuttles than I do." Nia released her hands from the flight controls.

"I trust your pilot skills more than mine. Besides, I can't hold your hand through life forever." Taona grinned and let out a soft laugh in a small attempt to lighten the mood.

Nia barked out her own laugh, then released a gusty sigh of relief. "Let's find a city farther away that hasn't been affected by the multiphasic pulse waves," she said.

"Fine, I am sure the Muak'Xod operate in every city." Taona's quiet, firm tone spoke volumes to her companion. "I release my now former life as a wife, stepmother, and Stadageo worker," she whispered. "I will make it through somehow and make it back to Ramah one day."

Nia nodded her head, commiserating. She took the controls of the shuttle, slowly accelerated, and then altered course using the distinct ridgeline of the Shebar Mountains as a guide to the Tevaroon region.

Nia stretched her neck, trying to loosen the knot caused by

14

the hard jostling of the crippled shuttle. She could see Taona was fatigued as well. "It looks as though we are not the only ones avoiding Perrapenta." About twenty kilometers ahead, the lights from dozens of ships flashed through the darkness as they descended to a myriad of small towns along the mountain slopes. "I wonder how many of those ships are government security forces?" Taona voiced her concern.

"The Overseers will have mobilized most of their intelligence agents in this sector of space by now. I am sure there is a very large bounty to hunt down and capture the perpetrators who destroyed the Stadageo, dead or alive." Nia swallowed hard. A wave of fear and anxiety threatened to overwhelm her. It was clear to Nia that Taona was fighting to maintain her own poise.

"Yes, I know that, but have you forgotten? We have been adopted into the family clans of Xongol. We are now going to use that to our advantage to make our escape off Letalis." Taona lifted her chin and caught Nia's gaze. Nia saw determination in her companion's eyes, and felt a fresh resolve settle over herself. "We have no time to lose in making contact with the Muak'Xod. Hopefully they will help us obtain a ship capable of reaching Ramah."

"Ramah, home…" Nia whispered the words, slowly savoring them. This was the first time they had felt the freedom to speak about it, lest their true identities were discovered. Her eyes began to water as homesickness that she had not experienced in decades welled up from the pit of her soul. She swallowed the hard knot in her throat, in an attempt to keep the deep sorrow contained. Like a scab ripped off a wound, her heart ached anew for her mother and father. A memory of herself as a child jumping into her father's arms broke through the mental barriers she had erected long ago. A stream of warm tears flowed as she groaned, deeply weeping the loss of her parents and siblings.

"Nia, control your feelings," Taona said in a firm tone. "We need to stay focused on our mission." Her words shored both of their defenses.

A green beacon on the control panel lit up. Nia straightened, patted her damp cheeks dry, briskly coughed, then opened up the communication channel.

"This is Euraxa Transportation Hub Control. Identify yourself," the male voice demanded.

Nia leaned closer to the communications link. "This is transportation shuttle STS three dash sixty dash five making an emergency landing. We have power core failure and are operating on emergency energy reserves," she said in a strong forceful tone.

"Make course to hub zone eight." The man's heavy Mulasain accent was native to the physically muscular humanoid race.

"Our auto-navigation systems are offline," Nia replied. "I need visual markers." As she spoke, she maneuvered the shuttle to a lower flight path.

"Just a moment... Head to hub zone twenty at the southern edge of the city. Your landing platform will be ringed with red lights."

Just then, chaos erupted loudly in the background. The man's voice cut out.

Nia's knuckles whitened as her grip on the controls tensed. "Hub control, are you still there? What's going on?" she asked, knowing full well that the destruction had reached this far region already. It was important for them to act as normally as possible in the situation. "Hello...please advise!" She let a thin thread of alarm ring in her voice.

"There was some sort of systems failure at the Stadageo." A wave of static hit her ears, causing her head to jerk back. Beside her, Taona's head did the same. "Control out." His voice sounded muffled, and the sudden quiet made it clear the connection had been cut. Nia switched off the com link. The earlier emotional outburst seemed distant as they began their approach to their landing site.

"Over there, thirty degrees portside," Taona said.

Nia exhaled. "I see it." She smoothly turned the small craft toward the large red circle of lights. "I hope our plan works." She couldn't hide the pessimism in her voice.

Taona pressed her lips together. "The way you stepped up just now reassured me that you will be able to carry through with the next phase of our mission," she said with confidence. "We'll do just fine."

"Oh, do you have the gift of foretelling?" Nia asked, raising an eyebrow.

"Just pay attention, will you!" Taona grumped back and shook her head with obvious frustration.

As they neared the landing hub, Nia spotted a dozen unoccupied lit circles and targeted their descent onto one of them. They silently watched support personnel scurrying around other ships that had just landed below. Their crippled shuttle on a last burst of power landed hard, jolting their already strained bodies. Popping noises erupted from circuits and acrid smoke began to fill the bridge.

"Are you ready?" Taona, not waiting for a response, swiftly deactivated the safety harness and stood up holding her hand over her mouth and nose.

No, I am not ready, Nia thought, a bit resentful. But she quickly followed suit. She bit her bottom lip and briefly held onto Taona's sleeve as they made their way through the thick smoke and out of the shuttle. Just ahead of them, a transport ship was expelling its passengers. The arrivals were met by security personnel who had an air of aggression about them.

"This is transportation hub security. Please remain near your ship. This is a level two quarantine order." The loud, automated instruction echoed in the somewhat chaotic emergency landing area. "Non-compliance will result in your immediate detention." The announcement repeated itself once more.

"Well, this is not good," Nia said in a low tone without moving her lips. The landing platform was flooding with more security and medical teams that were moving containment and treatment mobile stations around. Technology specifically used for radiation poisoning.

As if she sensed Nia's apprehension, Taona reached over and touched her sleeve. "Don't worry, we will get out of here," she murmured. "Just follow my lead." She took a few steps toward the exit, but a Letalis military officer accompanied by two soldiers with weapons drawn intercepted them. Recognizing Taona's and Nia's

Stadageo insignias on their uniform collars, the soldiers lowered their weapons to their sides.

"Is there a problem here, Captain?" Taona wore her authority very well, looking at him with piercing eyes. "Isn't that radiation scanning equipment?"

"There is a possibility you may have been poisoned by radiation if you were just near the Stadageo." The officer quirked an eyebrow. "Were you headed back to report for duty?"

Nia felt Taona tense at her side and bristle. "No, our shuttle systems failed because of an explosion of some kind," Taona snapped, using her rank to muscle him. "We did not have enough power to return to the Stadageo, much less to find out what happened."

"What type of radiation could damage our shuttle's systems?" asked Nia. She gazed intently into the officer's eyes, waiting for an answer.

"We are not exactly sure what type of radiation this is, only that the source has not been contained as of yet." His brief statement seemed truthful. "Something happened at the Stadageo." He seemed to come to a decision and motioned to a medical technician, catching his attention. The officer pointed at the two women. "They need to be scanned," he ordered loudly and immediately a medical team made their way over to them.

At least the scanning only took a few moments, not long enough for Nia and Taona to protest.

"We detect no injuries. They only have negligible traces of unknown radiation. I strongly believe they pose no threat of contamination to the population," the female medic said resolutely. She was already looking past them.

Nia grunted in frustration, drawing Taona's gaze. A number of security guards were standing behind makeshift barriers, waiting for the new passengers to disembark.

"Go to the next ship, and repeat the process. We need to evaluate and examine everyone who lands here." The urgency in the officer's voice sent the medical team scurrying on to the next group of individuals.

"If you need a place to stay until your ship is repaired, you may go to one of the temporary shelters indicated on this city map. Here." He motioned Nia to receive something he was holding. She stretched out her hand, and he placed a thin metal disc onto her palm. "You are cleared to leave." He tipped his head sharply to the nearby exit, then turned and strode to the next group of arrivals.

Nia caught Taona's arm, pulling them both into motion. They matched the fervent pace of those around them heading toward the nearest exit. Nia moved alongside Taona as close as possible, not breaking stride. "Did you hear what that officer said about the radiation? It's not contained." The plaintive note of stress in Nia's voice was clear.

"Yes. I heard him," Taona responded quietly. She paused, and pressed her shoulder against Nia's, tipping her head sideways. "Activate the map."

Once they were sure they weren't being watched, Nia stepped to the outside of the stream of refugees and did so. Thankfully the holographic map was very detailed, and included demographics and other general data, even a list of local business establishments. "Let's keep moving."

After a few hushed moments, they passed by a shelter, then another. "Ok, turn here," Taona said in a hushed tone.

The two sisters walked slowly down a darkened alley and then another. "Let's see if we can find some kinsmen." Taona continued walking ahead, but stopped when she noticed she was alone. She turned back to Nia, whose face was aglow from the map. With a few long strides, Taona was back at Nia's side, surveying the quiet in the menacing darkness.

"Find businesses run by the Xongol clan members," Nia commanded softly into the disc. A small section lit up in blue near their current location. More than a dozen businesses with Xongol names were listed at the top of the map.

"Great, now hand me that map." Taona took the device, dropped it to the hard pavement, and crushed it with the heel of her boot. "It's best if we don't leave a digital trail of what we do or where we go." She kicked the pieces farther down the alley.

As they rushed onward, Nia took a moment to retrieve the rest of the protein wafer from earlier and toss it into her mouth.

Snow covered most of the unusually crowded marketplace in the early dawn's light as they left the dim alley. Nia assumed that most were stocking up food supplies just in case things got worse. She cupped her hands over her nose and mouth, feeling the chill of the whistling wind. Traces of white mist from her warm breath leaked from between her fingers. They both glanced upward, watching a multitude of incoming ships. Nia couldn't help envisioning that they carried victims of the Stadageo radiation.

"This way," she said, moving toward a sector sparse with businesses, carefully searching for obscure signs of their family's clandestine organization network. Nearing the outer perimeter of the open marketplace, the streets narrowed and it became obvious that outsiders rarely ventured here.

"I sense we are close…" Taona's voice trailed off nervously.

"Yes, I think we are." Nia stopped and tilted her head slightly toward the subtle marker at the corner of an alleyway that was easily overlooked by most.

"I see it," Taona said. Wordlessly, they both went in together side by side. They followed the curved alley until they reached a dead end.

"Now what?" Nia whined with her hands on her hips. She kicked her boot into the snow in frustration. The question hung in the air for a moment. They looked up at the tall walls that surrounded them.

"I have a strong sense we are being watched," Taona said quietly. "I feel a malevolent presence nearby. I wish I had a weapon." Nia quirked an eyebrow encouragingly at her. "Ok, here goes nothing." Taona took a breath and spoke louder. "I am Taona Xongol and this is Nia Xongol. Our husbands serve on the board of Regents in Perrapenta. We seek opportunity to serve our family clan."

Just as Taona's last word echoed in the space, a beam of green light scanned them and then just as quickly vanished. In front of them, meter-wide metal rails rose up from the floor with rows of green glowing dots.

"Well, I think someone heard you," said Nia.

"Let's see where this takes us." Taona's tone wavered a little with a thread of fear.

Nia's lips were tight; she felt the same uncertainty of what they might encounter. She shored herself up with reminders of what they would face if caught by the Overseers. They stepped onto the small platform and gripped the bars firmly. The floor seemed to drop out from under them as the small elevator sped downward. Nia gritted her teeth in discomfort as it felt like her body lifted off the floor and her stomach dropped to her toes.

Tipping their heads back, they could still see the pale moon between the clouds in the early morning light just before the trapdoor closed above them. The air whistled as they went deeper into the ground, but thankfully the platform seemed solid and soon slowed until they bumped to a stop at the bottom. The lights of the chamber were as bright as day and the warm air was stale.

"Greetings, Taona and Nia Xongol. I am Dukar Gruppa the Muak'Xod, leader in this sector." A short human male spoke as he approached them. Behind him were four imposing and heavily armed men.

As Nia and Taona stepped off the platform, the metal rails retracted into the floor with a hiss. Both women felt trapped, vulnerable, and they folded their arms across their chests defensively.

Nia cleared her throat and spoke for them both. "Greetings, Dukar Gruppa." They bowed slightly in respect and waited.

"I know who your husbands are and we know that you have been assigned to the Stadageo project for years. We have eyes everywhere, especially on family." He grinned, revealing his small stained teeth. "You mentioned you want to help your clan."

Nia hoped that Dukar Gruppa did not suspect them as the saboteurs. She was well aware that the criminal organization would manipulate and use anyone to further their schemes, no matter who they were. "We saw the entire city of Perrapenta lose power. Taona has some medical background and can help not only our families but others as well if we can reach them. We will need a shuttle to do this. Ours was destroyed." She breathed through her mouth as an unpleasant waft of dank, musty air hit her nostrils.

"Yes...." He drawled knowingly, making it clear that he had been tracking them. "That is certainly admirable, your desire to help our family I mean." He cocked his head to the side and his beady eyes bore into Taona's, then Nia's eyes. They maintained a calm air, though they were wary of where this was going. "But the city is currently under a level one quarantine, due to the approaching lethal radiation cloud." He folded his arms across his chest.

"We need to reach our family and get them out." The rush of reactionary words pelted out of Taona. Nia nodded in agreement, quickly masking the look of horror she knew showed on her face.

She caught a spark of glee in his eyes before he quickly veiled it. *Does he know?* Her eyes narrowed in suspicion as they waited.

"It is impossible at this time even for us to attempt any rescues without detailed information on the current situation in Perrapenta." Dukar Gruppa paused, letting his blatant manipulation sink in deep. "It occurs to me that you could gain access to classified governmental reports that would help us to make better decisions regarding the safety of all our families and other individuals important to us." He pressed his lips firmly together, as if he knew he'd made his case and they wouldn't argue.

"I believe I can help you with that." Nia was very confident of her abilities. She narrowed her eyes, and with her own brand of manipulation continued. "There is a big risk for us, so we will be expecting the ship as a favor from you in return. I know that you can easily provide that for us."

He nodded once in acceptance, then lifted his right hand in the air to emphasize his point. "Of course it is of the utmost importance that you not speak to anyone regarding what you see or hear related to our organization, the Muak'Xod." His grin faded and was replaced with a cold, lifeless stare.

Nia and Taona glanced at each other and as custom dictated, they prepared to recite the oath they'd learned when they married into the family. Placing their hands over their hearts, they spoke as one. "I swear on our family's name and blood that I will adhere to the customs and dictates of the Muak'Xod, Dukar Gruppa."

"So you have sworn and have vowed on your and your family's blood." He raised his right hand, palm outward, accepting their pledges. "Good, now come with me." Gruppa gestured for them to follow him down the ramp.

The four armed men moved behind the sisters as they went down a dimly lit passageway. Nia and Taona lifted their hands to shield their eyes from the glare of bright light as they passed through a nano-wall. The multilevel small, military-style center was fully staffed with operatives. It was clear it was some sort of intelligence gathering center, as it was crammed with visual and audio stations. The equipment looked very expensive and high grade, but seemed to have been damaged as many access panels had been removed.

Gruppa dismissed the bodyguards with a wave of his hand. It was clear from their cold dismissive stares and flared nostrils that the guards held an intense mistrust of Nia and Taona.

One statuesque human female agent with high slashing cheekbones and slightly broad shoulders stood, and approached them.

"Sir." Her alto voice was respectful.

"Report." He grunted.

"We are still unable to break through the Letalis government's main security protocols. Also, there is no word from Drugah or his unit." She glared in cold challenge at the two new arrivals.

"Not good, they are most likely stuck in Perrapenta like everyone else." He crossed his arms, then came to a decision. He pointed to a well built, but unremarkable looking humanoid male agent standing a few meters behind the female agent. "Assist the others preparing for evacuation." Then he turned his gaze back to her. "You as well, Nephanor."

"Yes, sir." She glanced once more at the sisters, then followed the other agent already heading toward an oval-shaped tunnel.

Gruppa waved for them to follow him, then moved to her station. "Our core network of systems has been inoperable since the Stadageo was destroyed by an unknown energy wave." The sisters dared not look at each other or him and stared at the screen in front of them, waiting. "This older station is the only one that is still somewhat operable. So, if you can get me access to those classified reports..." His tone was demanding, yet Nia didn't miss the underlying, controlled panic.

She removed her protective winter headgear; her thick shiny black hair uncoiled and settled just below her shoulder blades. "I need access to the system," she said, her mind already racing on how to infiltrate the system without being detected.

Gruppa leaned over the station, entering a series of codes. "There you go." He watched intently as Nia navigated the labyrinth of government system cores.

"The Stadageo must have sustained severe damage to have released large quantities of radiation." Taona's mild comment seemed like a side note, but Nia knew it was designed to provoke him to confide information. Taona did not look up from her review of the data displayed on Nia's console.

A sharp snort drew their attention. "Damaged?" Gruppa cocked his head to the side with a derisive look on his face, then in a snide tone stated, "The Stadageo is in complete ruins. There is nothing left. The intense heat turned most of the area into heaps of radioactive rubble."

"We did not know." Nia managed to keep most of the strain out of her voice. He nodded once and placed his gnarled hand on the edge of the station.

The sisters briefly glanced at each other with veiled eyes, then focused on the screens, analyzing critical information regarding weather patterns. They grimly watched the black radiation alerts for all the municipalities in the region.

"Yes, here we go," Nia said. She used well-rehearsed false identities as she navigated through several data banks of the Letalis Citizen Volunteer Centers. "Hhmmm, the LCVC's civilian organization is in actuality an emergency auxiliary military reserve. I am sure you are not surprised, Dukar Gruppa," Nia said the last bit quietly, and continued her search.

Taona sat down next to her and began to look at the region's weather and the movement of the radiation contamination cloud on the area.

"According to this, there is a code red calling those in the LCVC registry to immediately report to their designated area and wait for deployment," Nia said. "No other details are given." She anticipated Gruppa's response and split the display screen into several sections.

"Let me see that report." Gruppa was silent as he read.

Taona's gasp was loud, drawing both of their heads in her direction. "The spread of a concentrated cloud of black radiation has not been contained. The estimated death toll is three point seven million citizens and…" She stopped speaking as a rush of emotion choked her into silence. She bowed her head and a flood of tears streamed down her cheeks, rolling freely down her neck.

"No." Nia's soul exploded with a terrified cry of despair and remorse. Her hand flew to her mouth and her face crumpled in grief. A single tear ran down her cheek, and her chest heaved with emotion.

Dukar Gruppa stood silent for a long moment. Then he said softly for their ears only. "There is nothing we could have done for your husbands and families. I am truly sorry for your loss." He awkwardly patted Nia, then Taona on the shoulder, clearly uncomfortable with the genuine sympathy he had just expressed. "Taona, your husband Siak was an important individual in our organization. He was well respected." He coughed, then his expression became impassive once again.

"Our families." Taona placed her hand on Nia's back and met her pleading eyes gently. After years living with adopted families, their emotional ties to them were as strong as they were with their families back on Ramah.

It was beneficial that neither of them had ever had biological children in these marriages, because of their revenge mission and the added responsibility that little ones would bring. As taught by the monastarium schoolmasters, they'd learned to control their reproductive organs and chosen to become infertile. Now they were thankful they'd done so; the thought of losing children they birthed would've been too much to bear.

A long moment passed as the sisters reeled at the news. Nia's whole body grew numb, but then just like she had when she lost her mom, dad, and siblings in the infanticide on Ramah, she shoved the anguish deep into the recesses of her mind and reigned in her emotions.

Now two of their families had been killed, these by their own hands.

"What about the black radiation. Where is it heading?" Gruppa asked Taona.

"It's called Cremindraux radiation," she replied slowly in a dreadful tone. "It's headed..." Her voice trailed off as she recalculated its direction. She cleared her throat and said in a flat tone, "Along the Shebar mountain range. It will eventually reach the Tevaroon region."

"How long do we have until it reaches us?" Gruppa asked bluntly.

"It has already reached the southernmost regions of the Shebar mountain range. It will arrive in the Tevaroon region within two days," Nia answered, staring at the Muak'Xod leader's solemn face. She had heard rumors that those who held the position of Dukar were not easily moved by fear. It had been ingrained in him to remain impervious despite the situation.

"Can you give me a more precise time?" His stoic expression did not waiver as he waited.

Taona swiveled her chair back to face the screen and entered more equations. She swallowed hard and swiped her palm across her eyes. "By tomorrow night, a new storm front approaching from the east will move the Cremindraux radiation toward us much faster." The grim statement hung in the air.

Gruppa's body stiffened, which spoke of a higher level of concern than his facial expression revealed. "We need to evacuate our immediate families and the rest of our clansmen who live here and move them to a safer place, like Kramatau. I doubt the radiation will reach the other side of the planet."

"Dukar Gruppa, we know that our husbands will likely not survive. But what about my children? Not all of them work in the city." Nia's voice rose with hope.

"Your children work in the town of Chamma. If they are as smart as I think they are, they will be headed to a more secure location—say, Kramatau." Gruppa nodded to convince them that his assessment was true. At Nia's receptive nod of agreement, he continued. "Well then, it looks as though we are finished here. I appreciate your assistance," he said, solemnly looking from one to the other. "You should go to the capital as well and search for your surviving family members there. If you would like, I can provide transportation, but..."

He paused, gazing piercingly into their eyes as if searching for something. "I assume that because you have high security clearance in the Stadageo project, you possess some fundamental understanding and knowledge of the realms beyond this one, and to a greater degree, the metaphysical sciences." He cocked his head to the side, then said. "So I would like to offer you a proposal to consider. One that would greatly benefit me, and of course entail a very handsome reward for yourselves. Before you decide to accept or refuse my offer, you must allow me to show you something first. If you are not interested, you can leave for Kramatau through that door over there." He pointed to where a Muak'Xod agent was just vanishing into the wall. "There are several small transports you can use if you wish. This is payment for your recent assistance." He paused momentarily to gauge their interest. "But, if you want a

31

vastly larger reward, follow me now."

With that said, he turned and headed down the ramp.

For the briefest of moments they looked at each other, but they already knew what they must do.

Chapter Two

NECROPIS

Concurrently, on the planet of Necropis, was the trio of wayward sisters who had also acted upon the signal given by Victoria and Balese. With precise timing, they had strategically placed explosive devices in predetermined locations throughout the redundant safety systems of the Stadageo.

As planned, Fay Sinadendra had made it to the local mining town of Gathmesh, a spirited sector located several hundred kilometers east of the Stadageo. She made her way down a public walkway she and the other two sisters had used several times during their planning. Her destination, the Red Horn Tavern, was marked by a half-lit neon sign that flickered in the dawn's early light. Using her gift of spiritual discernment, she searched ahead on her path for danger and for those who preyed on the weak and unsuspecting.

Several security guards stood at the entrance, watching those who entered. Once she passed them, she was lit by a dark green beam of light as she walked nonchalantly through the dimly lit entrance. A three-dimensional holographic image of her AR-57 energy pistol holstered on her hip floated a meter ahead of her. Above it was the same word in several languages, *Allowed*. Fay adjusted her outer vestment, which clearly marked her as a member of the Choshek family clan. This as such offered another layer of protection. She proceeded to the third level dining terrace.

To remain inconspicuous, she ordered food and watched the six-armed chef masterfully chop and dice a variety of plants while he simultaneously cut the saltwater catch of the day. He placed roasted pieces of it into a small steaming cauldron that smelled delicious. Her stomach unexpectedly growled. She reached into the inner pocket of her overcoat and retrieved a coin made of precious metal. Glancing at it, she said in a tone that rose slightly over the din of the room, "This should do it." She flipped it over the narrow counter at him. One of his hands snatched it out of the air mid-arc. "Keep the change," she said with a smile.

He nodded in gratitude, placed the fragrant bowl in front of her, and then smoothly transitioned to help the next customer. Fay gripped the handle of the small pot and made her way to the edge of the terrace.

She felt the glances and stares of patrons as she wove through the labyrinth of those seated and others milling about. Fay felt a bit unnerved and timed her gaze back at them, conveying that she was not an easy mark. Near the terrace ledge she found a small table and flipped open her overcoat as she sat, to expose her holstered pistol to any would be assailants. Occasionally, bursts of humanoid laughter mixed with the sounds of other sentient beings echoed out into the open space of the terrace. As comfortable as she could be in the current circumstances, she began to eat the broiled Selsha fish stew, one of her favorite seafood dishes. Her eyes closed briefly in pleasure at the sweet aroma. The scent was a short reprieve from the more pungent odors of the exotic dishes preferred by those dining around her.

The rogue sisters had frequented establishments like these, where unsubstantiated rumors and propaganda abounded. Like the one about the rogue elements of the Marium Kahnet in the Malgavatta galaxy, who supposedly had established formal ties with the Krauvanok Alliance. *How could that be? Sister betraying sister...and for what? Did they forget what happened to our families and loved ones on Ramah? How far we have fallen.* Fay could not accept those rumors and dismissed them summarily.

Her thoughts turned to a possible future to someday fall in love, marry, and maybe have children of her own. Occasionally, she gazed at the wide spectrum colored lights of the mining complexes along the Medeo Mountain ridge on the horizon, then nonchalantly surveyed the patrons leaving and arriving, on the lookout for Mirinda and Orisa, in between each mouthwatering spoonful. A cool breeze from the mountain range swept across the terrace. A half a kilometer away, a dozen cargo ships were lifting off carrying payloads of precious raw materials, like Barraxium ore used to build and repair the Stadageo. The entire region was enveloped by naturally occurring electromagnetic fields created by the densely packed rare ores. The metals hampered most terrestrial listening devices, providing a great place for shadow operatives.

Fay had just taken another spoonful of her stew, when the lights flickered and then cut out all at once. Streaks lit up the sky as the raw material transports dropped in simultaneous succession, crashing into the unforgiving mountainside and erupting in balls of fire.

An eerie silence fell upon the terrace.

They did it! She exulted silently. *I hope it takes them a long time to repair the Stadageo*, she thought, gloating. Guests around her began to panic and rush out of the tavern. On high alert now, she took the last drink of her Kravajava.

A frown touched her brow. *It's past dawn. They should be here by now.* Her body stiffened and she rose, looking for a safe way out. Waiting any longer was not an option. As agreed, she would go to the secondary location in Ausertane and wait for them there.

Mirinda brushed her thick, curly red hair away from her sweaty face. Her body ached with pain. She closed her eyes, and with the training she'd received as a youth examined all of her major organs. "Good, no internal bleeding or major damage," she said quietly, relieved that her added strength and recuperative abilities were due in large part to her consumption of Cymbratar.

In one swift motion, she shot to her feet, then nearly crumpled as another stabbing pain struck her right side. She leaned her head against the ship's bulkhead, wincing. With teeth gritted, she tentatively touched her lower rib cage area. "Must have fractured at least one rib," she grunted without moving.

She pivoted her head against the cold metal, staring at the now closed cargo bay door, which had opened when the ship violently crash-landed. The force of the impact had flung her into the storage hold full of equipment. The door had then closed behind her, sealing her in. "Let's see how quickly my rib will heal." She groaned heavily as the stabbing pain gripped her right lung.

The lights flickered annoyingly, in a dizzying fashion. Curling trails of smoke from burnt ship components wafted in the cool air. It was clear she had been unconscious for a while, as it was eerily quiet. She reached into her utility belt, retrieved a single red oblong-shaped Cymbratar gel tab, and gratefully swallowed it down her irritated throat. Out of the three sisters, she had been the one who'd outlined most of the workable contingency plans. It was she who had suggested they not take the restorative gel tablets more than once this year to save the other in case of an emergency.

The pain began to ebb. She breathed a deep breath, testing it, and felt a surge of power flood into her muscles and bones. The next breath she took was pain free and she gustily exhaled, relieved. Pushing off the intermittently vibrating bulkhead with her hands, she composed herself as best she could. Stepping into the now chaotic cargo area, Mirinda pushed over containers and other items as she reached the door.

"Let's see here..." Mirinda glided her hands over the disabled control panel and removed the thin metal faceplate. Energy sparks shot out as she slowly pried it off. She blew a focused stream of air and waved her hand to fan the acrid smell of burnt metal and other toxic fumes away from her face. Mirinda, as always, had prepared for every eventuality, and reached into her side pocket to retrieve a spare Choshek stylized barrette. She quickly gathered her voluminous red hair into the traditional fashion of her adopted family clan. The sporadic lighting stabilized to a low setting. She pressed her ear to the cold cargo hold door, hoping to hear signs of life on the other side. "Too thick," she hissed, slapping the door with her right palm.

"Ok, let's try this again, shall we?" Her stalwart character would not let her give up hope. She pressed her face up to the small opening of the control panel and reached as far in as she could with two fingers. "Ouch!" She waved her burnt fingers in the cool air and jumped back from a fresh wave of smoke that hissed out of the opening. Her frustration growing, she ripped a thin tube that had popped out from the panel and flung it toward the rear of the cargo hold.

She froze when she heard a small splash. "Wait, water!" she exclaimed in surprise and immediately went to investigate.

Crouching over the puddle, she lightly touched the surface with her fingers. She lifted them to her nose and smelled. "Salt water." Alarm rose and she quickly quelled a sense of panic. "We must have crashed into the sea." Her mind raced to find another way out of the cargo hold.

Just then, the heavy cargo bay door squealed as it began to open. She was relieved to see the reptilian fingers of Alborz Mirza, a fellow passenger she had just met, wedging farther into the small opening. He was prying it open with raw strength. She heaved a big sigh, thankful it was just a large enough opening for her to squeeze through.

"Are you alright in there?" Alborz said in a low breathy voice typical of the Lacerta race.

"Yes," she said, as she carefully wedged her body through the narrow gap, all the while surveying the main passenger section of the transportation shuttle, searching for Orisa. Mirza's beautiful multicolored scales gleamed even in the dim lighting.

"I saw you disappear behind the door, just as I hit this wall upon impact. Are you injured?" His caring tone seemed genuine.

"A few bruises, but I am doing well, considering." She looked into his multifaceted eyes and forced a smile to reassure him. "Have you seen the other human female who was with me?" She brushed at the black smudges she felt on her cheeks with the back of her hands, observing a number of the alien passengers at the ship's main doors struggling to pry them open to no avail.

"She is up in the bridge." He pointed a long clawed finger in the general direction. "I believe she said something about rerouting some power to open the shuttle doors for us to escape?" His nictitating membranes briefly closed, moistening his large blue-green eyes. "I believe we've crash-landed on some rocks near the sea cliffs." He raised his nose and his dark red tongue lightly flickered out, scenting the air. "I detect traces of sea water inside the ship."

"You are right," she said quietly, not wanting to alarm the others. "The cargo hold is slowly flooding."

His imperturbable countenance was unreadable. "I need to check the cargo hold to see if maybe there is something we can use to escape this death trap. I don't want to be around when sea predators arrive." Mirza turned toward to the cargo bay. "Can you help me open this a little wider? Maybe I can find something useful in the cargo containers." He looked as if he might get stuck as he wedged his much larger frame into the narrow space, with his large palmed hands pressed against the door and his back against the door jamb.

Mirinda sat on the floor, grabbed the edge of the open door, and readied herself. "Now…" he said, pushing against the door with all his might. The veins in Mirinda's neck pulsated from the strain of her exertion. The doors popped open and they remained momentarily motionless.

She looked up to meet his gaze. "I hope you find something we can use to get those doors open, Mirza." Mirinda reached for his extended scaly hand and he easily lifted her to her feet. He bowed slightly and she watched him go into the cargo hold.

The transportation shuttle shook suddenly. Mirinda grabbed a nearby seat and stared out of the oblong viewport. The dim light of the coming day confirmed that they had slipped farther into the sea. Panicked sounds came from the passengers packed tightly at the jammed doors, still frantically trying to get them open. A renewed sense of urgency flooded her mind and she quickly made her way up, then across the walkway to the bridge.

The slight tang of the cool salty ocean air wafted in the cabin as she approached the partially opened access to the bridge. Using both of her hands, she pushed the door open quite easily, to her surprise. She entered and stared at the remaining stars twinkling through a ripped portion of the hull of the bridge. The edges were like sharp blades, far too dangerous for anyone to pass through.

"Orisa, where are you?" Mirinda yelled, looking around from side to side. In her haste, she almost tripped over one of the two pilots who had died in the crash. The other pilot was just beyond his seat near a spilled open medical kit. Her slim alien body was in a fetal position, partially covered in a shimmering web-like mesh, as was the way of death of the Etreago race.

Mirinda heard a noise near the shattered viewport, and carefully made her way over. She raised her voice to be heard over the air rushing through the bridge. "Orisa, is that you?"

"I am under the main control panel." Orisa's muffled voice came through, and Mirinda placed her hand over her heart, deeply relieved. "Stay where you are... Don't move while I am try to reroute the main power to the..." Orisa's words were drowned out by the loud noise of power surging through the ship. The lights flickered back on.

A mild shock jolted through Mirinda as she noticed a sharp metal beam jutting out from the floor. She was glad she'd taken Orisa's advice to not move. The pointed tip of the beam was stained with the drying green blood of the Etreago pilot.

"I saw you were thrown into the cargo bay and came straight here to get the power back on." Orisa's voice was still muffled. "I guess you found a way out." Her hand appeared on the charred edge of the main control panel and she gracefully emerged. Her oval, black-smudged, tanned face was wreathed in a smile. She was the youngest of the three sisters.

"You look very tribal, sister." Mirinda tipped her head to the side "I do approve." She gathered her in for a brief hug.

Orisa shook her head disapprovingly. "Uh," she lilted. "Are you injured?"

"I broke a rib, but the Cymbratar I saved for an emergency healed it." A loud scraping noise echoed throughout the ship, reminding them of the peril they were facing. "Sea water is leaking into the cargo hold," Mirinda said hurriedly, loud and clear over the whistling sea winds. "We are slipping into the ocean. We need to get everyone out now!"

Orisa looked over at the partially operational main control panel. "We may just have enough power to get the doors open," she said and activated the emergency shuttle door release function, and the cold air outside blew in. "Let's get out of here!"

They both ran off the bridge.

Just then they were jolted off balance as the ship was rocked by a large wave. After regaining their footing, they followed the other passengers off the empty ship and carefully traversed along jagged rocks, occasionally leaping across large spaces between them. Along with a few others, with Mirza among them, they made it to the largest and highest cluster of rocks that jutted out of the sea. The bright sunlight revealed a myriad of ships had also crashed along the rocky coastline. In the distance, the flat nose section of a large transportation shuttle floated above the waves. A group of individuals at the edges was quickly moving to the center of the partially submerged ship.

"Do you see that?!" Mirinda's voice rose with fright. "There, about a hundred meters away to the left." She pointed urgently at the open ocean, which was splitting apart as something rose from the depths.

"Yes, I see it. I believe it's a Pegadreth," Orisa said with certainty. Mirinda was well aware of Orisa's love of the ocean. She had shared many times her fascination with sea creatures, which had begun as a very small child.

"I hope they eat only sea plants." Mirinda couldn't help the thinness of her voice. She was thankful it was muffled by the crashing waves against the rocks they were standing on. She started to count the bobbing heads in the water, but stopped when they were wrenched under one by one. The cries of those atop the nose of the transport reached them, carried by the wind.

"Oh, no!" Orisa yelled and grabbed Mirinda's arm.

The hairs on the back of Mirinda's neck rose in horror as she watched a male Pegadreth with its many-horned head and neck raise its upper torso out of the water to a height equal to that of the nose of the shuttle and smash mightily against it. She couldn't look away and gasped as one of its four large clawed appendages penetrated the ship's hull, and some of the people clinging to each other slid off. Their screams of terror ended abruptly as they plunged into the sea and were immediately devoured by fifteen-meter-long flying Sea Scorphins. The rest of the survivors met the same fate.

Mirinda and Orisa stood in shock, watching the dim flashing emergency beacon vanish as the ship sank under the water's surface.

Orisa leaned closer to Mirinda. "Let's hope that someone is looking for these ships," she shouted into her ear.

Mirinda, still staring at those churning blood-stained waters, came out of her paralyzed stance with a jerk of her head at the yell. She finally turned away, saddened to the depths of her being at the loss. A moment later, she grabbed Orisa by the hand and pulled hard.

"What? Oh…" Orisa's eyes widened as she saw a small craft was floating to a narrow tall rock two hundred and fifty meters beyond them. Suddenly, it was engulfed in a sea of white foam as it was forcefully lifted out of the water. Their mouths dropped open in awe and everyone around them gasped in fright. "Carrasaurex." Orisa mumbled the word.

The mighty apex sea predator had taken hold of the small shuttle with its massive claws and ripped the nose of it away. Its wide, menacing mouth clamped down with a loud snap on a handful of doomed passengers.

Suddenly, the Carrasaurex was rocked to the side as it was hit by a volley of high-charged energy blasts from a Necropis military ship descending from the sea cliffs. Even so, it refused to let go of its prey, clinging stubbornly. But another volley of fiery blasts finally forced it to relinquish its hold. With a sharp rotation, pushing the remains of the shuttle against the rocks, it vanished beneath the waves.

"Look," Mirinda said, tapping Orisa's shoulder and pointing to the ravenous creatures circling their downed ship. Orisa reached out and squeezed Mirinda's hand tightly. There were more ships slowly making their way along the cliffs to their location, but would they get here in time?

Just then, a large shadow cast over them and their silent cries of grief turned to joy and elation. A hovercraft was descending to rescue them.

Mirinda and Orisa, along with the rest of the shuttle survivors, arrived at a military base near the Necropis capital city of Magiathep. The base was full of activity; many survivors were being guided to one of several temporary shelters to receive medical care, and no doubt to be interrogated. Small metallic spheres methodically glided over the heads of every individual in their party, scanning faces with green beams of light to identify them. Everyone was then separated and divided into groups. Military personnel in clearly marked radiation vestments, pushing medical equipment, approached each group in an orderly fashion. The sisters remained focused and kept their wits about them, for fear of being discovered as the perpetrators of the destruction. It took a lot of skill to keep their composure as the military personnel came closer and closer. Their fear deepened when they noticed a group comprised of high-ranking Stadageo administrators being escorted to an adjacent building about one hundred meters away.

A military commander came and stood in front of their group. He perused his data pad then stared piercingly at Mirinda and Orisa. "You two," he barked loudly. "Stand over there with them." He pointed to three other Stadageo workers huddled together looking bewildered.

The sisters moved quietly to join them, strongly feeling the coming danger. As their group swelled to ten, Mirinda noted that the group had varying degrees of Stadageo high-level security clearances. She swallowed hard, keeping her face and body calm and relaxed. *Not good.*

The commanding officer turned his gaze to the remaining cowering group still seated. "Report to that building directly in front of you, for debriefing," he said sharply. "Do not deviate, go now!" He sternly pointed to a large structure with his gloved hand. They did as they were told, escorted by a dozen soldiers.

The thin-faced, middle-aged officer turned back to them, placed his hands behind his back, and began to pace in front of them, glaring at each person. His piercing look and hostile demeanor were designed to unnerve and intimidate. "You will come with me for debriefing." He stopped pacing. "Fall in," he commanded the military guards who bracketed the small group on either side, with weapons held at the ready.

Mirinda kept her eyes on the back of the tall man in the line ahead of her, focusing on containing the dread that reverberated through her. *Breathe slowly, carefully, and evenly. They don't know.* With a small movement, she looked around her. *None of this is normal protocol for Stadageo emergency response. They are taking us to the same building they took the previous high-ranking Stadageo administrators. Not a good sign.* With each step they took toward the nondescript large gray building, Mirinda couldn't help but believe their end was near.

The building's wide doors opened, allowing the group to enter, then slammed shut behind them.

"Halt." The officer raised his hand, then spun and faced them. "Mirinda and Orisa, step forward," he said in an emotionless tone. As they moved forward, they were surrounded by soldiers. "Escort these two to room 4B." He reviewed the data pad once more, dismissing them.

"Follow me," said one of the soldiers.

The spacious modular unit's air was as cool as it was sterile. It was only furnished with seating for the various life forms, now filled with Stadageo workers. The doors closed behind them and with a hiss of air sealed shut. They were trapped now. They slid into seats as instructed. Five heavily armed guards, with the impervious shielding over their faces masking their expressions, moved to stand in front of them. It was yet another intimidation tactic. But as that felt familiar, the sisters ignored it, waiting for what would come next. A tall humanoid male in Krauvanok military intelligence (KMI) clothing came through a door to their left, and surveyed the room until he found his next subject.

"Orisa Sotasen, step into this room." His metallic, reedy tone echoed around the silent room. Without hesitation, Orisa stood up and gracefully made her way to the waiting interrogator. His thin nostrils flared as he looked her up and down. Gesturing silently with his arm, he ushered her into the small room beyond the doorway.

Mirinda watched her disappear, her heart thudding.

The room Orisa entered stank with the sweat of fear from its previous occupant. The door slid shut and a dark cloud seemed to descend around her. She looked up into the pale countenance and solid black eyes of the two and a half meter tall KMI officer.

"Orisa Sotasen, please sit." The talon-like nails on the tips of his fingers exaggerated their length as he touched the surface of the table. She repressed a shiver, noticing a smudge of blood on his index finger. She felt the intimidating power of his merciless gaze as she heard him whisper words in Toxrokk—dark speech. As directed, she sat on a wide metallic bench, which lit up with cascading shades of blues and greens. "Place your right hand on the table, and do not remove it until I say so." He remained standing as he reviewed the data displayed on a screen atop the table near him.

"Tell me," he said with a slight hiss as he leaned forward over the table, looking deeply into her eyes. "Did you cause the destruction of the Stadageo, or know someone who did?"

"No, I did not. Who would do such a thing?" she said in a low authoritative tone. "We crashed into the sea after our transport lost power." It was a maneuver designed to redirect his attention. "I am thankful our military rescued us, or I would be dead." She stared innocently into his eyes as best she could, using all of the techniques she had learned back on Ramah.

"I see you are originally from Gehenna, yes?" His skin gleamed wetly in the humid room.

"After my family was killed by the Mantis Alliance, I moved away to start anew to forget my past. Which I have done," she said calmly. He peered closely at the screen, watching for signs of her guilt. For what seemed an eternity, he entered commands and stared fixedly at the screen.

Menacingly, he braced his hands on the edge of the table and bent toward her. "You will remain here on base for further questioning." His lip curled up with disgust as he continued, "Your family will be informed of your stay." Dismissively, he waved his left hand over the bottom of the screen. "Remove Orisa Sotasen, and place her in the security holding cell sector three," he told the guards who had just entered the room.

Turning back to her, he bared his long sharp teeth. "I believe you are hiding something." His face twisted momentarily with hate, and he huffed out. "But I assure you, I will find the truth. As you know, all traitors are summarily executed." He turned to the soldiers. "If she resists, or tries to escape, you are authorized to shoot to kill." The barked orders were as cold as his stare. "You will stay there until our investigation is completed sometime tomorrow." He stood motionless, observing the guards flank her still seated on the bench, steaming that she was not cowed.

One of the guards pointed his energized weapon at her. "Get up and come with us." Orisa detected a thread of anger in his voice. She stood and made her way in front of them. Silently, the second guard prodded her with the tip of his weapon out of the interrogation room, through an opening that was previously hidden by a masking field. She winced at the force of the intentional blow. She snapped her head around to get her bearings over her right shoulder, but only saw the glowing point of the lethal weapon. "Move it!" he yelled.

She was alone now, wasn't she? She felt defeated. The clanging of their footsteps was loud in the wide corridor. Above them hovered a small metal sphere that followed them to a door, which slid open, then shut behind them.

"Stop," said the previously silent guard in a quiet, calm voice. Orisa turned and faced them, ready to fight. They had deactivated their shield visors, revealing they were human. "You must follow us if you want to live." The other guard had his back to them, peering around in every direction.

"What is going on?" she asked. He leaned forward slightly and moved the collar of his uniform until she saw the small mark of the Choshek brotherhood. *My clan.* A flood of relief made her feel weak for a moment and she looked at him with burgeoning hope.

"I can't go into detail right now, but I will tell you that all of those with high security clearances in the Stadageo project are being detained in level one security sector three right now. I know for a certainty they will all be executed tomorrow. No exceptions."

She sensed in her spirit that what he said was true and shivered reflexively. "What about Mirinda?" she asked.

"Don't worry about Mirinda. She will join you shortly. I will explain everything when we are safe. So I need you to keep up with me. We will be moving very fast from here on out," he said, and reactivated his shield visor. The other man had already moved ahead and opened the door leading outside.

Heat waves caused by the mid-day summer sun emanated off the surface of the various military vehicles and ships. They briskly walked past a row of small transportation craft, some of which were being loaded with high-ranking Stadageo administrators. *They are going to be executed tomorrow.* Grief tightened her throat at the thought.

They entered a vehicle near the security perimeter fence from the middle row of transports. The lead Choshek agent removed his helmet, placed it under his left arm, and then touched the tip of his index finger to his lips after the loading ramp retracted behind them. She understood that there were listening devices in every military vehicle. He motioned with his hands that they were to jump off the craft at the appointed time. The two agents who had been masquerading as guards quietly removed all of their body armor and stood proudly in their Choshek agent desert attire.

The door slid open as the craft glided along the outer perimeter of the base by the sand dunes. He again motioned for her to follow him as he then leaped out of the open hatch. She watched him tumble and roll onto the red sand, then stop his forward momentum with grace and skill. The other agent tapped her on the shoulder. It was her turn. She had no choice.

Grimacing with determination, she leaped out of the craft just as it began to pick up speed. Her feet hit the sand hard, awkwardly twisting her ankle. She yelped as she pitched forward, burning her palms on the hot sand. Sand sprayed on her head and shoulders with the impact of the second agent's very large, heavy body landing so close to her. In pain, she looked up as the craft sped up and vanished out of sight, preprogrammed on autopilot to return to its previous location.

Without saying a word, the lead agent reached down to a thick rust metallic band around his waist and touched several symbols on his utility belt with his fingers. Ahead, a mirage of water appeared and vanished quickly as the cargo door of a small ship materialized thirty meters ahead. Orisa limped after both agents as fast as she could, trying to keep up. The younger and larger of the two turned back, scooped her up, and carried her unceremoniously onto the ship.

Chapter Three

TARTARUS

Gandu Khanon sat in his quarters and enjoyed the fruit of his labors. His heart swelled with the pride of his accomplishments, as his ship convoy neared their destination and the center of the Leviathan project, the Mecropex.

Without warning, he was thrown hard into his oversized chair with such force it nearly toppled over as it slammed into the wall. The crystalline cup flew out of his right hand and shattered on the metal floor. A second jolt violently threw him off the seat, and he skidded across the grey floor face-first. He came to rest right on top of his favorite red drink. The acidic beverage stung the cuts on his face and he roared in anger. The lighting in his quarters flickered momentarily, then a ship-wide, automated emergency message came through the wall speakers.

"Warning: High levels of radiation detected."

He carefully placed his hands in a spot that did not have any shards of the broken Tethromak cup. "Toqesh Nah Salal," he said, and immediately felt the familiar power coursing through his hands as he was smoothly lifted to his feet. He clenched his fists then opened them near this face. "Duramesh Soulshav." His deep voice resonated strongly around him. The sting of the cuts on his face diminished and soon vanished, leaving only dried blood.

It surprised him that no one had immediately come to check on his wellbeing. But more disturbing than that was the continuous low sound of the ship-wide emergency message repeating itself. He noted the stale air as he sped over to an experimental long-range communications platform. The top section of the table moved as if it were alive, tripling in thickness. The singular thick base parted into three evenly spaced reptilian fingers, with razor sharp talons protruding up through the tabletop. The talons glowed with power and discharged energy into the center of the table, creating a large liquid sphere with three crimson bands equally spaced apart. Energy pulsed from the three talons into the sphere. Khanon stared in wonder at this new technology that allowed a duplicate of one spirit to be projected across great distances. Appearing within the energized orb was the life-size image of the Krauvanok Alliance Overseer and his peer, Adad Mahoth.

"Gandu, I could not reach you earlier. We have lost contact with the Mecropex." Khanon reeled in shock. He didn't bother trying to hide his reaction. Mahoth continued, "The initial multiphasic energy wave caused by the destruction of the Leviathans' primary power source interfered with the Erebus sphere functionality. The shock waves were so powerful that they damaged planetary and orbital communications. Unfortunately, all powered propulsion systems were victims as well. There have been an untold number of casualties. Don't worry about your family's safety, they are being taken to the Basillex compound, along with my family." Mahoth paused to allow the information to settle.

Khanon released an angry breath, then in a strained tone inquired, "What is the damage to the Mecropex?"

"We are not sure. Our initial analyses indicate massive discharges of multiphasic energy. We have determined it was caused by the destruction of the multiphasic matter fusion reactors on Pratheous... We don't know what happened to the Mecropex, yet."

The veins on Khanon's head pulsed with murderous rage, and purple and blue tendrils of energy erupted around his tightly clenched fists. He understood the ramifications if that were true. The complete destruction of the underground facilities on Pratheous would most certainly affect the Mecropex, but to what degree he wasn't sure.

"What about the Stadageos on Letalis and Necropis, have they been attacked as well?" He wanted to believe that the Mantis Alliance was responsible for the damage rather than the infiltrators he had been warned about by Abbadon. His soul silently shrieked in terror, for his life might now be forfeit.

"I have not received any word with communications down, but I have already contacted Kravjin High Council about this incident." Mahoth's anger was evident in his harsh tone. "I am certain if it was an attack, the Krauvanok Alliance will respond accordingly!"

He contacted the High Council. That does not bode well for me. Khanon clenched his fists at his sides, as his terror was replaced by anger and unmitigated hatred for the Marium Kahnet. *We should have not let one survive. Next time I will make sure they are all dead!*

"What is the status of your ship and that of your fleet?" Mahoth asked.

Khanon lifted both hands to the ceiling and the room filled with Toxrokk incantations. "I can see there is considerable damage and loss. You will have to send assistance to secure my ships." His concern for his ships and their precious cargo subdued and replaced his anger. *Even with my project destroyed, I can rebuild a Mecropex with the Hedropex Spheres.* The thought of having to rebuild from scratch was not a pleasant one, but it might spare his life.

"I foresaw the need for assistance." Mahoth's tone held a slight edge of impatience now. "I sent ships to your location before I contacted you. They should reach you at any moment. Now if I may, I have other matters to attend to, Khanon… Mullgoth."

Khanon responded in kind with a sharp bow. The communication platform returned to its previous state. A noise at the door caught his attention. "It's about time!" he said bitterly. The metal door to his quarters was forced open. A medical engineer and two officers entered swiftly. Before he could ask any questions, they were upon him.

"Lord Khanon, are you injured?" Zora Mindendra, a high-ranking KMI officer, asked with brusque concern. Her high cheekbones were highlighted by her short, neatly combed hair. She reminded him of his own wife in so many ways. Intelligent, cunning, and lethal.

Thelvisha, a short, stocky Txon female who was the senior physician on the mission, waved a handheld scanner over his chest area. "I do not detect injuries," she said with relief. "I see blood, where are you hurt?" She cocked her head to the side, peering closely at his face, then began to blot at what looked like wounds. He jerked his head back, not wanting the attention.

"I assure you, I am as healthy as I was twenty years ago." He impatiently waved them away, annoyed at Thelvisha's continuous medical device scans. "Give me some room," he said irritably and sniffed. He straightened his Overseer vestments and stretched his shoulders back to emphasize his robust health. "Now, give me a concise report on what has happened."

"Lord Khanon, we are using auxiliary power for the main shields while repairs are being made to the primary power core regulators. Master Engineer Cermus is currently overseeing the work," volunteered the young energy science engineer, Wei.

"What is the status of the Hedropex sphere containment module?"

"It is secure for now, but the closer we drift toward the multiphasic vortex, the more unstable the containment will be." Wei's answer brought a wave of fear that washed over them all.

Khanon bit out, "Multiphasic vortex." It took all his will to maintain his composure. "What is the status of the other ships?" he continued through partially gritted teeth.

"We have a line of sight on four of our ships. A fifth burst into a cloud of bright red energy as it entered the vortex." Wei's tone was high and fearfully thin.

"I will have to assume the sixth must have been destroyed before that." Khanon noticed the room getting colder. He shivered. *Environmental systems must also be off line... Can this get any worse?* He brought his racing thoughts to a halt.

A crackle in the ceiling speakers preceded an announcement from a monotone voice: "Attention all personnel, report to the medical center to receive radiation inoculation. The ship-wide multiphasic radiation contamination is now approaching critical levels." The ship lights changed to a red hue, denoting the danger they were in.

"Are the transpods operational?" asked Khanon.

"Yes, Overseer," Wei replied.

"Good, I'll take that bit of good news." Khanon reached into his vestments and retrieved four Cymbratar tablets. He handed two to the young man. "One is for you, the other for Cermus. When you start to feel weak or nauseous, eat it. Inform Cermus the same. It is imperative that the main power be brought back online. Now go." He waved him away.

"Here." Khanon gave Mindendra and Thelvisha the remaining tablets.

"Thank you, Lord Khanon," said Thelvisha, tucking the highly coveted substance inside her uniform.

"You may return to the med bay." He snapped his fingers in dismissal.

"Yes, as you command, Lord Khanon." The lights flickered as she strode through the door, leaving an eerie dark shadow in the room.

"Warning, shields at thirty percent," blared a mechanical female voice.

"I need to be on the bridge. Let's go," he said to Mindendra urgently. He watched her lightly shiver at his side as the dark cold entity that always accompanied him touched her malevolently.

Captain Draxrad, in the midst of chaos, was busily working at his command station on the bridge. He didn't look up to acknowledge Khanon. "Warning, shields at twenty-five percent," blared the mechanical female voice.

Khanon lifted his hands to the ceiling once more. "Thakus Nosso Metta!" A fine black mist appeared around his hands, and enveloped him in a transparent shadow. He slowly lowered his arms to his sides, walking calmly toward the captain. *This will give me an added measure of protection from the radiation.* He noticed an inquisitive look on Mindendra's face as she remained near the door. He smirked at the all too common reaction to his dark power. Through the main viewport, he clearly saw three ships in the distance.

"I was informed there were four ships!" His loud, angry voice broke Captain Draxrad's concentration. With great composure, the battle-experienced commanding officer turned to face him. His thick, singular silver eyebrow emphasized his large bronze eyes that held a great reserve.

"The fourth has met the same fate as the other two ships, Lord Khanon." His deep voice was calm despite the frantic activity swirling all around them. "We are doing all we can in order to avoid the same." Fearlessness was common in the Xebechet race's stoic nature.

"Continue to do what you can, Captain." Khanon was reassured by his steadfast demeanor. The captain unceremoniously turned back to his duties.

As Khanon returned to Mindendra's side, he noted she looked mesmerized by the hypnotic pulsations of colored energies at the vortex's edge

"Beautiful, isn't it?" she whispered. Just as the comment left her lips, another bright red ball of energy engulfed another ship. "Is there any way for you to transport us or yourself to safety, Lord Khanon?" It was common knowledge that Kravjin could do such marvelous things.

"No, I have not reached that level of power yet," he said, lifting his fisted right hand in determination. "But one day, I will," he vowed. *If I live long enough, that is. I will reach the next level of Necronos transcendence very soon.*

"Lord Khanon." Captain Draxrad's sharp tone broke his musings. "We have company, opening communications now," he said calmly.

"Greetings, Lord Khanon. I am Captain Falco, of the Krauvanok battle cruiser *Prakus*." The life-size holographic image flickered atop the communications table. "Fleet Admiral Adraxes is currently securing Tartarus as we speak and coordinating with the Krauvanok Alliance fleet command to secure Letalis and Necropis from a possible Mantis Alliance invasion." The captain's age looked to be early thirties, quite young for someone of his rank.

"Greetings Captain Falco, your arrival is a welcomed one. As you can see by your external scans, our ship's main power is offline. We cannot engage our engine drives. What is your assessment of our situation?" Khanon sensed that he would have to leave the ship taking the special and unique power source, the Hedropex sphere, with him.

"Your shields are now at twenty percent—" Captain Falco started.

"Warning, radiation has risen to critical levels," the warning systems interrupted the conversation.

Annoyed, Khanon motioned with his index finger across his neck in a cutting motion to Captain Draxrad. The captain immediately deactivated the automated warning system.

"Our team of engineers has reviewed the damage to both of your ships. We have determined that the engine drives can be repaired within two days." Falco's words were just as he feared.

"It's obvious that I don't have a choice here." He went with his earlier gut reaction. "We don't have time for repairs. We have to abandon both ships, now!" Anger swelled deep in the bowels of his being as he uttered the words. *I won't lose everything now. I won't...*

"Excuse me for a moment, Lord Khanon." Captain Falco turned his head to address a subordinate. "Commander Atabascae, prepare for recovery of crewmen aboard Lord Khanon's ship." His stern expression was obviously second nature earned on the battlefield.

"Lord Khanon, our long-range scans indicate no life signs aboard the second ship. They have drifted far too close to the anomalous vortex to attempt any rescue, in any case. Also, because of the dense bursts of multiphasic energies, we are unable to use the ship-to-ship Matter Transportation Portal. You will have to use the emergency escape shuttles," the captain said smoothly.

"Very well, Captain Falco," he replied in kind, but internally, his spirit writhed in anger. "Once we are safely aboard your ship, we will return to Tartarus immediately!" His threatening tone was not lost on those around him. They knew the danger they were all in if his wishes were not met.

"Yes, Lord Khanon." The holographic image vanished. The lights dimmed on the bridge.

Captain Draxrad caught his angered gaze. "Lord Khanon, please make your way to the emergency escape transports. My lord, I must stay behind and release each transport manually. I believe I will have just enough time to make the last transport in time."

Khanon smelled impending death in the uncirculated air. "Are you sure it can't be done remotely?" Captain Draxrad responded with a single negative shake of his head.

Even as he acknowledged the oncoming doom, his spirit refused to let go of his precious cargo. It took the overwhelming force of self-preservation to release his tight grip. "Very well, Captain Draxrad. I will see you on the *Prakus*. Here, eat this when you feel the effects of radiation." He tossed the captain a Cymbratar gel tab and gave him a nod of respect in light of the rare heroic courage the captain was exhibiting.

"Let's go!" he barked, spun around to face Mindendra, and brushed hastily past her, leaving the bridge.

Captain Draxrad activated the emergency escape transportation codes into the ship's core systems. With regret he made the ship-wide announcement. "Attention all personnel, this is Captain Draxrad. Your orders are to abandon ship. Report to your assigned escape shuttles. We are transferring to the Tartak battle cruiser, *Prakus*." He cleared his voice, then continued, "All personnel, report immediately to the emergency evacuation transportation platforms." He repeated the command once more, then the ship's automated abandon ship sequence started.

The captain pragmatically watched the last crewman leave the bridge. He continued to manually open the individual escape hatches to allow the shuttles to leave.

Suddenly, a strange hissing, a whisper of unintelligible words behind him made him freeze in his movements. He spun his head around, but saw no one.

"This must be the effects of radiation poisoning," he said aloud, trying to stay calm. "Nevertheless, I have to open the remaining hatches." He felt a twinge of nausea, and consumed the tablet Khanon had given him.

As he made his way over to a partially damaged control panel, he saw transparent serpent-like beings gliding around the bridge. He was not afraid, merely curious. *Maybe being this close to the vortex and consuming Cymbratar is causing this strange visual effect.* Setting the thoughts aside, he rerouted all remaining power, including life support, to stabilize the multiphasic containment module power regulators.

As he did so, more and more strange, unrecognizable words and sounds echoed around him. His heart pounded ever fast, but he did not stop.

Khanon and Mindendra crossed over a short span connected to one of the dozens of platforms harboring the emergency escape transports. "I'm glad that I replaced the emergency escape pods with class three military transports. They have sufficient shielding to protect us as we travel to the *Prakus*," Khanon said aloud with some pride.

"Excellent foresight, Lord Khanon." Mindendra's voice held a note of hope. "It looks like no one will be left behind."

He paused, looking at the rows of shuttles being boarded by hundreds of personnel. He waited for her to enter into the transport ahead of him. The lights turned off inside the retrofitted Chevka battle cruiser just as he entered. He felt a burgeoning sense of loss, as though a part of him was being left behind, as the door slid closed. But he quickly composed himself, and briskly led the way to the bridge.

He noticed she looked sickly. "Take your Cymbratar, you don't want to risk damaging vital organs."

She slipped her hand into her vestment, retrieved the Cymbratar, and carefully placed it on her tongue. Like most non-critical project personnel, she had never been issued Cymbratar, until now.

They were greeted by two humanoids as they entered the bridge.

"I will fly this transport and Intelligence Officer Mindendra will be the co-pilot," Lord Khanon announced. "You two will man the auxiliary stations." He stood impatiently, waiting for them to move out of the way.

"Yes, Lord Khanon." The older of the two stated. "The shields are activated at full strength." They hastily moved to their new posts.

Khanon settled himself in the uncomfortable seat and entered the coordinates to the *Prakus*. The small vessel lifted off the platform to join the others exiting the various open hatchways that dotted the doomed battle cruiser's hull. As they approached the *Prakus*, he looked in vain for his other ship. His entire body tensed with the fresh realization that yet another of his prized ships had been lost.

Affected by the roiling vortex in the distance, the navigation soon failed. He had no choice but to deactivate the autopilot. Aided by the *Prakus* Matter Polarity Beam, the crippled transport was drawn into a large cargo bay. From his vantage point he saw many hundreds of other shuttles disgorging passengers. He powered down the shuttle. In the ensuing silence, Mindendra and the other two remained in their seats until he departed the vessel.

He was not surprised to be met by dozens of Tisradeen soldiers sent to formally welcome him, as the high-ranking Overseer he was. A senior officer greeted him at the bottom of the ramp. "Welcome aboard the *Prakus*, Lord Khanon. I am Security Major Gureck. Do you need medical assistance?"

Khanon acknowledged the captain's salute with a sharp salute in return. He could see an approaching medical team. "We do not. However, I must speak to Captain Falco immediately."

The major nodded and turned to the medical crew. "Go to the next group of passengers over there." He pointed to a group of bewildered people standing ten meters away.

Major Gureck barked out dismissal orders at the formation of the Tisradeen soldiers, then turned back to him. "Lord Khanon, please follow me."

Khanon motioned to Mindendra to accompany him, then stopped in his tracks as he caught sight of her. Somewhat startled, both he and the major stared at her for a moment. Her face was aglow with a youthful radiance and natural beauty. "You do justice to Cymbratar," Khanon remarked.

"This way, Lord Khanon." Major Gureck broke the momentary lapse and they strode ahead.

They felt the antigravity dampening fields shift as the doors slid closed behind them in the large transpod. They stood silent, not looking at each other.

Khanon closed his eyes, and was attempting to clear his mind with all of his might, when the dark protective mist around him vanished. He sensed it even with his eyes closed; anxiety set in, and he felt he was missing something very important.

He opened his eyes to see that the lights on the side panel had stopped blinking. The grey transpod doors opened, announcing their arrival to the combat bridge. Although the bridge was full of activity, their presence did not go unnoticed. A single high-ranking humanoid male KMI officer dressed in very distinct military vestments approached them. His unique rank insignia identified him as a Grand Inquisitor. "Lord Khanon, welcome. I am Thygan Kruel. I am pleased to inform you that all of your crewmembers are now aboard. With the exception of Captain Draxrad, who has refused to abandon his ship as expected." Kruel's imposing frame dwarfed most around him. "Captain Falco will meet you in a moment." Kruel turned his cold, merciless black eyes on the lower-ranking KMI officer. "Officer Mindendra, I expect a full report by this time tomorrow, understood?"

"Yes, sir," she replied, standing tall at attention. Although she was assigned to an Overseer, she was still bound by the rules and protocols of the Krauvanok military command.

Khanon to a lesser degree was also subject to them. Kruel turned back to the Overseer. "Lord Khanon, I believe you will most likely be summoned to report to the Krauvanok Alliance Supreme Command council to give an account regarding this incident." His hard voice reminded Khanon of his own on occasion.

"I agree with your assessment, Grand Inquisitor." Khanon respected the KMI Officer's unfeigned loyalty to House Krauvanok. Especially one with Thygan Kruel's rank and position in particular.

"If you will excuse me, Lord Khanon, I must continue on with my duties."

Khanon's nod dismissed him.

Captain Falco immediately made his presence known with a brief salute and greeting. The middle-aged human male was typical of a Krauvanok high-ranking military leader, excelling in both tactical and political genius.

"All are on board and accounted for, except for one person." Falco waited for his response.

"I understand the duties of ship's command, especially of those in your position, Captain Falco. But let's give him a little more time." Deep inside, Khanon knew that he would not see his trusted captain again. This was a fresh blow to him, as Draxrad was someone he'd handpicked years ago to pilot his ships.

"As you wish, Lord Khanon." With a raised brow, Falco motioned broadly. "You may sit at the command platform with me if you wish." He turned to the side, gesturing with a nod for the Overseer to proceed first. They settled in the command seats.

"Avisha!" Khanon muttered strongly with clenched fists, suddenly remembering his niece had been in Mecropex when it was destroyed. The captain looked at him inquisitively but said nothing. *What am I going to tell my brother, that his daughter's death is due to traitorous infiltrators?* A well of sadness began to swell in his troubled spirit. The loss of his favorite niece, who had been like his own child, was devastating. She had been so promising, so dedicated to him and brilliant.

With his spirit roiling in torment, he watched the ship with Captain Draxrad drift closer to its destruction. Everything blended together at that moment, the years of planning, his hopes and dreams wiped

67

out in one fell swoop. He gritted his teeth so tightly they almost cracked under the strain. *I want to kill every single Marium Kahnet.*

Captain Draxrad's upper body lay over a charred control panel, as his life was slipping away. His ears twitched; he heard something behind him.

"You will not perish. Take and eat...you will not die," said a sibilant voice.

Gathering every bit of his remaining strength, he lifted himself up and saw on the communications platform a large thick round wafer made of a black substance. He staggered over and leaned heavily on the platform. *I am so tired.* With his arm feeling like lead, he pulled the offering over and felt a wave of coldness wash over his arm.

Peering through dim eyes at it, the center of the symbol resembled the Kravjin emblem, but was different, with strange red letters encircling the edges. With nothing to lose, he put the wafer in his mouth. It was so sweet and immediately his belly warmed.

Then, a searing fiery pain like nothing he had ever felt before struck him. His teeth locked together and he doubled over as every muscle and tendon contracted and convulsed. He fell to his knees screaming in agony, but there was no one to hear. The pain eased slightly and he lifted his head to look out the bridge viewport just in time to see the bow of his ship disappearing in a shimmering veil. His head bowed and he closed his eyes, waiting to vanish from this life.

A few moments passed and nothing happened. Feeling marginally better, he opened his eyes and rose to his feet in a rush, amazed at what he saw.

Khanon held his breath, waiting for his ship to explode like the others had, but it did not. It simply vanished into a shimmering veil just inside the multiphasic vortex. He closed his eyes, feeling the loss deeply; it fed his hatred. He shoved all emotion aside and, coming to a decision, he turned his attention to Captain Falco.

"Proceed to Tartarus, Captain Falco," he commanded in a flat, hard tone.

The captain immediately ordered navigation to engage full thrusters. The distance began to grow between the concentrated multiphasic energies and the *Prakus*. When they were far enough away, the main propulsion system was engaged, which immediately propelled them to light speed.

Khanon sighed gustily with relief, then reached into a pocket and retrieved the Cymbratar gel tablet. He casually put it on his tongue. As he did so, he pondered. *Why didn't my ship explode like all of the others? Did Captain Draxrad figure out a way to re-engage the main power cores to restore the ship's shields? I will have to solve this mystery so that I can salvage not only the Hedropex spheres, but my reputation and my life!* The image of Avisha rose in his mind, interrupting his thoughts. *I will avenge you Avisha, I promise.*

He looked out the viewport with unseeing eyes, just barely registering the multicolored spectrum of colors that erupted around the ship as they traveled faster than light speed.

Avisha Khanon stirred from the darkness. Lying flat on her back with sulfur burning her nostrils, she felt as if her head was in the jaws of a large carnivore. Her face contorted with the agony caused by her injuries. She sat up, but immediately regretted doing so. Streams of warm tears ran down her cheeks as she bit down on her lip from the pain and tasted blood. In despair, she wailed childishly.

Gulping in a large breath, she grimaced, trying to get a grip on her emotions. She began to take slow, shallow breaths of the humid and acrid smoke-filled air.

Suddenly, panic struck her again, as the noise of tearing metal rocked her body violently. Just then, she felt the power of a cold presence all around her. This lifeless dark entity immobilized her. Panting in fear, she peered into the darkness and could make out a large, beastly creature just beyond the dark shroud that she was wrapped in. It spoke, but she could not understand the guttural sounds it was making. The cold emanating from the onyx veil pricked her skin; she frowned at the smell of death trying to enfold her. Then an even larger entity, with what seemed to be molten lava for veins, appeared.

"Avisha Khanon, Lord Saurcine demands your presence."

Before she could respond, a frightfully huge, scaly black hand grabbed her upper torso, sending a shock wave of pain throughout her body. She went limp, instantly losing consciousness.

Chapter Four

LETALIS MOON

Victoria Maja's soul wrestled with remorse and guilt, as she struggled with the information she had just received from her mercenary captor, Raduu. The Stadageo on Letalis had been completely destroyed, releasing concentrated clouds of deadly radiation across large populated areas. Millions of lives had been lost; entire cities had been decimated.

I am sure that if Balese and I had known the scope of the devastation, we would have altered or abandoned our plans altogether. The remorse in her spirit grew apace with her thoughts.

But it was already done.

Without any particular reason, she focused upon a strangely shaped raven perched across the mostly barren canyon. *The incalculable quantitative destructive powers from the realms of Creminmorta, released by the machinations of the fallen state of creation, whose corrupt seeds build on the blood stained altars of death.* Victoria transitioned into a semi-meditative state as she felt the mild warmth of the sun on her face, *The Eretsalok. The sea of eternal fire, where the power of death and suffering will be sentenced to reside for eternity's future. Where Kravanoblus, his conspirators, and those whose lives are fed by corruption will also be cast into.*

"As the book of Kodashah says, this takes place just before the age of Eloyshib." As the whispered words left her parched lips, the thin, almost transparent blond hairs on her arms stood up. "Why, and how did I get here? Is this to learn the error of my ways?" The despair in her voice spoke volumes of her shame and regret.

Still seated at the cliff's edge looking across the canyon, she occasionally inspected her right wrist where the Nazar band had fused to her DNA and bone. She had already thrown the Nazar covenant ring down into the canyon. "I wonder if I will ever be able to remove this cursed band," she said mournfully, with her head drooping in despair. A movement down on the canyon floor caught her attention. A half-dozen red and black-haired grazing animals moved to an island of vegetation. Her mind was fatigued from the endless speculations. She sighed and cupped her chin in her hands with arms braced on her knees. Her body ached from sitting in the same position for most of the morning. She found herself staring repeatedly at a particular formation in one of many ravines in the distance. She had tried to dismiss it, but every time she gazed back, it became less obscure, until she finally concluded that it was not natural. Her stomach grumbled with hunger, but the unsolved mystery surrounding her transportation to the Letalis moon and her culpability for the deaths of millions of civilians had suppressed her desire to eat. With her acute hearing, she discerned the light steps of two people approaching.

Em and Tola came into view around a large boulder. "Here!" Em said forcefully, flinging a small metallic container toward her.

She easily snatched it out of the air. It was clear by the sloshing sound it made it was fluid. *Most likely water.*

"Thanks, Em." Her voice held the dark weight she felt. She twisted the cap off, and brought it to her lips, drinking deeply. "Kravajava," she said in thanks, enjoying the lightly sweet cool rejuvenating liquid.

"You will need more than that to sustain you." Em reached into her pocket and tossed Victoria a Tisradeen Energy Protein Pack, a combat ration used by Krauvanok Alliance military. "You have not eaten much since you got here." Her voice held a note of concern.

Victoria gratefully took the packet, pulled it open, and took a bite, still staring across the canyon at the object in the ravine. "When is Raduu expected to return?" She looked calculatingly at them. She could only hope that her descriptions and the names of Nia and Taona would expedite their safe capture.

"That is difficult to say." Em sank to a comfortable squat with her lips pursed. She followed Victoria's intent gaze to the ravine she was looking at. "There is a level one security net around Letalis. I am sure that these two moons have been scanned by the Letalis military by now. Thankfully we have a masking field around this plateau." Em's tone was factual as she returned her gaze with some curiosity to Victoria.

"Well, you better hope and pray to your god that Raduu finds them before the Overseers do." Tola's disdainful tone spoke volumes of her dislike of the sisterhood. "I hear they have already executed hundreds of those involved with the Stadageo projects." Victoria's calm demeanor did not waiver at her somewhat provoking tone as she continued to stare across the canyon.

"Are you looking at anything in particular?" Em was now openly curious at what would hold Victoria's attention for so long. Still crouching, she pivoted to peer in the same direction.

"Yes, as a matter of fact, there is an unnatural formation just inside that ravine near the large red outcropping. About three kilometers away." Victoria pointed across the vast craggy-dry landscape.

"I don't see anything, just rocks and patches of vegetation," Tola remarked.

"Which one? They all look alike," Em said skeptically with her eyebrow raised.

"It's slightly darker than the rest of the area." Victoria pointed again.

"Ah, I see it now. Something about it does look out of place, I'll give you that." Em touched the side of her headgear, activating her visor. Tola followed suit.

"I don't see anything out of the ordinary." Tola snorted then said, "I think you've been in the sun too long." She laughed at her own remark.

"It might be an abandoned mining post of some kind," Em speculated. "I am always game for seeking lost treasure. Along the way with other for profit activities, we have found considerable amounts of valuable items over the years," she boasted.

Tola snorted again, then reluctantly adjusted her visor. "Hmmm actually, I see what appears to be a grey metal surface of some type. It might be an entrance of some sort. The ravine narrows quite a bit, but it's large enough to conceal an old mine."

"If it's a mine of some sort, there could be valuables that were left behind." Em rose to her feet and put her left hand on her hip. "Raduu won't be back for at least another day," she reasoned aloud, as she continued to survey the ravine, and the canyon below. "It won't take us long to reach that area if we take that path to the right. We could follow the dry riverbed!" Excitement for the challenge thrummed in her voice.

Her enthusiasm was infectious and Tola immediately engaged in the plan. She looked upward. "We will have to wait until the orbital station passes to the other side of the moon."

"Agreed." Em deactivated her visor and glanced at Victoria. "What about her?"

Immediately knowing where this was going, Tola's glare of disapproval was revealed as her visor retracted. "She would have to come with us, of course." Her disapproving look would give pause to someone with less strength than Victoria. "Or we could tie her up until we return." She offered the option with some pleasure, then continued, "I prefer that." Tola's dislike of Victoria was no longer thinly veiled.

"I am willing to go with you." Victoria stood and dusted off her hands "As I told you before, I give you my word as a—"

Tola sharply raised her right hand with her palm outward, instantly changing the atmosphere of the conversation. "Stop!" Her voice seethed with hatred. "To me, you are no different or better than us. You are most likely responsible for the murder of countless millions on Letalis. Save your lies on how you got here and your self-righteous piety for someone else, sister!"

Victoria easily brushed aside the verbal assault; she was used to working alongside individuals who for one reason or another hated her. Some had even tried to sabotage her career. She remained deceptively calm, but ready to react if it got physical. "I am ready to go." she looked first at Em, then somewhat challengingly at Tola.

"We can't use our hover scooters," Em said. "They would be detected once we leave the masking field canopy." She lifted her hand and momentarily grasped the talisman that hung just inside her vestment.

"I believe we should find a way down on the other side of this plateau on foot. I think I saw a way down. Not an easy one, but a way nonetheless." It was at this point that it was clear Victoria had spent quite some time figuring out a way off the plateau. She hoped that this bit of transparency would gain some of their trust.

"So, you found a way down, did you? Even if you had reached the canyon floor, we would have easily tracked you down," Tola drawled. "But then, I think you know that." She smirked with an edge of sarcasm at Victoria.

Em looked at her mercenary partner. "Tola, I believe she remained with us because of her hope for a reunion with Nia and Taona." She looked at Victoria with a quirked eyebrow. "Am I right?"

"That is true." Just then she felt a rise of frustration so strong it threatened to upset her composure. She held back a more aggressive response that might've caused an escalation, leading to a scuffle.

It wouldn't end well for Em and Tola. "That is why I have given Raduu all the information I have about them." Her tone was blunt and hard.

"That might be true, but it does not change the fact that I do not like you or trust you... I am not intimidated by you either!" Tola spat back at her.

"We should definitely only take small arms. Any energy discharges larger than that would be easily detected by the orbital stations around Letalis." Em drew her AR-57 energy pistol and with blinding speed aimed it just to the right of Victoria.

"The Guyyians sure know how to create an exquisitely elegant, deadly weapon," Tola said admiringly. She turned to Victoria, then said, "Of course, you don't need a weapon. You have your training as a Marium Kahnet assassin. And your god," she added with a derisive smirk.

"Victoria..." Em twirled the weapon on her right index finger. "Lead us to the path down to the canyon floor you found." She gestured for Victoria to start moving with her palmed pistol.

Victoria's face was hard with determination as she brushed past them into a tall thicket of dry vegetation. They quickly followed, their passage marked by snapping branches.

It wasn't long before Victoria was a ways ahead, though she could still hear them talking behind her.

"Where did she go? She was just here." Em's voice was accompanied by the snap of a branch coming loose from the skeletal trunk of the tree.

"I hope this is not a waste of time," Tola grumbled. Her heavy steps crunched sound the dry, brittle branches on the gravel-covered ground.

"I'm sure we will find something of value, Tola. I strongly sense that!" Em said confidently.

"Well, you have had the uncanny ability to be right in such matters before. Hopefully, you will be on point this time too." Tola's left hand rubbed the talisman hanging on a metallic rope around her neck. It was the twin to the one Em wore. "You sense things, but I have great fighting skills," she boasted. "But really, where did she go? Can you see her anywhere?"

Victoria looked back through the branches and saw the panic in their eyes that they'd lost their captive. "I am over here," she shouted. She had already cleared the obstacle of petrified desert trees and was crouched at the edge of the cliff.

Their bodies scraped the ground as they slid down the smooth rock surface. Without uttering a single word, the three looked down into the canyon.

"I see another way down," Em said excitedly, pointing to a small ledge several meters away. "It looks to be less treacherous than the one the Victoria chose. There seems to be a little animal trail, just there." She spoke in a hushed voice as she peered over the edge.

Tola surveyed the narrow path. "Yes, Em, it does look more accessible. Victoria, do you think you can make it down unharmed?" Tola's deep alto voice was slightly mocking. "Raduu would not be pleased if you got injured, or even worse, killed."

Victoria knew that her emotionless, hard expression that had been carefully cultivated over long years first with Krav Naga lethal fighting skills and then as member of the Synogog was off-putting. She let the strength of her gaze be her only answer, staring at Tola with narrowed eyes. Tola quirked an eyebrow, then broke eye contact. Victoria felt a little better discerning that Tola truly was concerned for her safety, if only to reap the reward promised by the sisterhood.

"Em, I changed my mind. Something doesn't feel right about that path I think we should go the way Victoria found."

Em looked at Tola's stubborn-set face and relented. "Fine, have it your way. But I will go first then." She walked to the smooth rock's edge, some meters ahead. In one fluid motion she sat on the edge and pushed off, while holding onto the edge with her hands to slow her momentum, then let go, gracefully landing on the two-meter-wide ledge below. They carefully watched her position herself to land on the next ledge. "This next one is a little more difficult. I'm going to have to swing my body over. I think I can make it."

Em slid off, holding onto the sharp edge with her strong hands. They heard her grunt as she disappeared under the lip. A long moment later her voice reached them. "I made it, I'm going to keep going. Are you coming?"

Relieved, Victoria tightened her boot clasps and rolled up her sleeves, examined the distance of the ledge below, then stepped off the ledge. She skillfully used her hands on the warm rock surface to reduce and control the speed of her descent, and landed in a particular crouching stance, which was further evidence of a well-trained tactician.

Victoria could sense Tola's hard stare even through the impervious visor as she wiped the sweat off her brow. *Good, she will know by now not to mess with me.*

The three stood on the last crag several meters above the canyon floor, contemplating their only way down.

"I don't like it. This seems to be a trap of some kind!" Tola palmed her weapon and gripped it tightly, ready for any eventuality.

"I don't feel good about it either." Em was chewing on her lip.

Victoria crouched down and peered farther down the narrow ravine. "Quiet now, I see a small pool of water just inside a large cave. It must be fed by the river when it rains." Her sharp vision was as good as some nocturnal animals, due in part to repeated consumption of Cymbratar over the years.

"I still don't like it." Em reiterated her misgivings about going through with no way of escape. "Something doesn't feel right."

"I can go first if you would like," said Victoria.

"No, I will go," said Em firmly. "But I will need you to help me out."

Victoria wasn't surprised by Em's response, as there was a different feel about the place. Em sat on the edge of the rock terrace and slid her body off the warm, dark red rock as she stuck out her right hand. Victoria gripped it with both hands, gently sank to her knee, then laid flat on the surface all the while holding tight.

"I'm ready for you to let go." Em's voice echoed down the canyon. They heard the loud crunching of gravel as she landed on the canyon floor. Victoria looked over the edge. Em stood looking up at her and Tola with her weapon palmed.

"I'm tall enough to make it down the rest of the way on my own. But I think it best if I help you down, I don't want you to hurt yourself, sister," Tola said lightly in challenge.

Victoria didn't doubt that, looking at the two-meter tall, fit woman. *She could no doubt hold her own in a skirmish.* "No, I can manage." She sat on the edge, placed her hands on the warm surface, pivoted outward over the edge, and then briefly hung on it. A moment later she loosened her grip and landed gracefully on the rusty canyon floor.

"Do you see anything?" Em said, noting Victoria's intent stare into the dim space between the two canyon walls. The jagged rocks could slice them up if they weren't careful.

"I have pretty good vision, but I don't see or sense any danger." Victoria went down on one knee and discerned the area once more. She shook her head, then rose to her feet. "I don't see anything." The sound of Tola's heavy landing behind them echoed in the cavernous space.

"Still worried, Em?" Tola said as she moved to her side. It was clear she had heard their conversation. "I don't see any sign of danger. Maybe this time you are off. Do you remember Siminosis, our mission into the forests of Tillexia?"

Em's look of embarrassment made it clear she remembered.

"I will go first." Tola powered up her pistol and moved slightly ahead. "Victoria, you follow behind me, you are our payday after all." Her dismissive tone was unmistakable. "Em, you have our back. If there is any threat, we will be ready." She carefully set off. Just ahead was a short steep incline formed by rainwater run-off over a very long time. Tola gingerly stepped onto the slick surface.

Suddenly she lost her balance and with a few inept slipping and staggering steps fell with a hard crash onto the surface, which was unexpectedly slick with a viscous substance. Her short screech echoed as she slid down farther into the ravine.

"Stop, don't take another step." Victoria's stern voice resonated loudly, and Em froze. The sister moved in a blur, removing her thin overcoat, then plucking a blade from Em's utility belt, and swiftly split her belt into two parts and tied the two ends together. With one end anchored in her teeth she pulled, tightening it as best she could. The makeshift rope would have to work.

"Em, can you hear me?" Tola's thin voice was a relief to them both. "You were right after all, I am stuck in some type of trap. You need to be extremely careful. It looks like I'm near the lair of some sort of predator," she hissed, her voice laced with fear.

"Don't worry, we're coming down prepared. Hold tight and be as quiet as you can," Em said, sounding rather frustrated. "I do want to remind you that I said this was not a good idea." The low grunting huff she issued seemed to be her way of expressing disgust. "Let's hope you're not as helpless as one might assume, sister. What do you intend to do with that?"

Victoria ignored the question and tossed one end of the cloth rope to her. "Stretch this out as much as you can." Em tugged hard. "That should do it. Do you know what might be down there?" Victoria glanced at her briefly.

"Well, there are any number of apex predators in these types of environments throughout this region of space," she said with a disgruntled look. "None of which you want to encounter unless you are heavily armed." It was clear that Em, like most highly trained mercenaries, had vast knowledge of the various regions and environments in which they practiced their trade.

"So, your small energy weapon would have little effect against one of them, right?"

Em's grim silence indicated that her assessment was correct.

Victoria pressed her lips together and hurriedly scraped away large chunks of the slime off the surface for better balance. After a few moments, she said, "There, this should do it." The confidence in her statement emboldened Em to stand close to her. Victoria inspected her commandeered blade. "This weapon, if used properly, can do a lot of damage." Looking at Em, she could tell that she was plagued by fear of becoming a meal. Victoria instinctively knew she was the best choice to help Tola. "I will go down first." Em remained silent, acquiescing. "Just so you know, this is not my first time facing such a beast. I killed a Shevator on Tartarus when I first arrived in this region of space. It was ferocious and hungry, but I took it out with a blade." She figured talking calmly like this would help Em break out of her frozen fear.

"Very well, I will hold the end." Em wrapped one turn of the short rope around her right wrist, then gripped it tightly with both hands. She dropped to her left knee. Victoria, holding onto the other end, slid over the edge and lowered herself to a rock jutting out of the side of the canyon wall that was just below. She let go of the rope and looked up at Em, who was now on her belly looking over the edge.

Victoria noted that Tola was calm for the moment, but was trapped in what looked like a silken web. She followed the thin, sparkling, silk-like strands that clung to the wall. Some ended where piles of empty husks of animals lay. They were no doubt overtaken when they tried to drink at the inviting pool of water just beyond. The stink of death and decay was repulsive. "Tola, don't move, not even a hair." She looked back up at Em and put her index finger to her lips signaling her to remain silent. "Slide down, I will break your fall," she whispered.

Em nodded, then scooted on her belly over the edge, dangled for a moment, then losing her grip slipped. The force of her landing almost knocked Victoria into the web.

"This is not good." Em stood slowly, shaking her head, then crouched and in a slow spin with weapon drawn surveyed the area.

"Look over there, Em." Victoria's tight tone was soft but filled with warning. Palming the blade, she pointed twenty meters beyond Tola, where one of the legs of the beast poked out from a shallow cave.

"I see it," Em whispered, and pointed the pistol in that direction.

Tola was motionless on one knee, with one of her arms entangled in the amazingly strong, transparent silk strands anchored to a group of partially buried boulders. "Get me out of here!" she said through gritted teeth.

"This entire canyon is a trap, Tola. Did I mention we should have gone the other way?" Em's quiet voice was chastising. "We should have gone the long way along the other riverbed."

"Shut up, Em!" Tola said with a matching anger. "Get me out of here." She was fighting the urge to struggle her way out. "Is it an Enchangu, or Voosul?" A look of fear slid over her formerly stoic countenance. Her eyes grew round as she saw them take a step back.

"I see its eyes…" Em pointed with her weapon and shook her head in despair. "Those are the eyes of a …Terratak," she said with dread.

"Victoria," Tola said in a hushed whisper. "Take my weapon. When I try to get free, it will attack. You need to hit one of its vulnerable areas, like its spinnerets or its eyes if you can." She flung the pistol, which bounced off one of the boulders, clattering loudly onto the stone ground.

Without taking her eyes off the Terratak that still remained in the cave, Em reached down and picked it up, then tossed it to Victoria, who snatched it out of the air with blinding speed. This commotion finally caused the Terratak to move even farther out from under the crag, exposing its massive head and fierce-looking thick and red, armored mandibles. The three-meter tall beast with six spear-like legs changed color just then to match that of its lighter surroundings. Victoria's eyes widened. She had never seen this type of predator before.

"It's a risk we will gladly take," Em said through barely parted lips. "Just be ready to free Tola."

Just then the noise of an animal in distress filled the ravine with an unexpected diversion. Momentarily startled, the Terratak stopped moving toward Tola and scurried back into the cave. A four-legged grazing animal had lost its footing and fallen down the slick slope. It didn't appear harmed as it got up and began to bound away. It almost made it past the large crag where the ravening beast lay in wait. But then it got snared in the silken strands of a web and began to squeal loudly yet again.

In a flash of a moment, the predator's long pincers impaled the caught animal. Its sharp shrieks of pain pierced their ears and echoed pitifully down the canyon. The following eerie silence was broken only by the scraping of the animal's hooves rotating against the rocks as the web coffin was spun around its writhing body.

"Spinnerets," Em said, with some awe in her voice, pointing at the writhing back end of the Terratak blocking their escape. Its soft underbelly was exposed to them as it relentlessly injected its poison and liquefying fluids into the dying animal.

Tola slid her free hand into her utility belt and pulled out her jagged assassin's blade, and began to slice the strands from around her torso. Marginally freed, she reached into a side pocket and retrieved a small metal sphere from her utility belt, activated it, and tossed it at the Terratak's exposed backend. The force of the explosion sent Victoria and Em back hard against the boulder. But immediately enjoining Tola's efforts, they blasted away at the writhing beast.

They lost sight of it in a thick cloud of black and gray smoke. The deep, guttural noises of its wounded distress vibrated their bodies. Dust began to swirl in pulses with the beating wings of the Terratak. Its large shadow cast over them as it flew out of the ravine and disappeared, still crying loudly.

Tola appeared in front of them, plucking the remaining strands of the sticky web from her clothing. They sighed in relief. "I suppose a thank you is in order, so here it is…" She removed a hydration gel tab from her utility belt and tossed it to Victoria. Em popped one of her own tabs into her mouth.

"Do you sense any more danger, Em?" asked Tola, and Em shook her head. "Good, let's get going, shall we? "Before a probe comes to investigate." She reached out her hand to Victoria, silently demanding the weapon.

Victoria handed it over. "It's ready to go," she said, noting Tola's look of dawning respect.

Tola turned as if nothing had ever happened and strode toward the eviscerated animal, cutting through the silken strands as she ploughed forward with heavy confident steps.

The waves of heat from the midday sun shimmered just above the dry, cracked topsoil of the canyon floor. They quickly abandoned the route along the dry riverbed in favor of the path with patches of shade at the base of the canyon wall.

"I think we are very close to our destination," Victoria said, carefully examining the surrounding surfaces. "Look up there." She pointed above their heads. "Do you notice an odd shaped section of rock missing? Now follow the line all the way down."

"It travels directly to... there!" Em said excitedly.

"It looks like an old container of some sort. This whole canyon may have been a large body of water once and over long periods of time could have made those large impressions in the cliff's surface." Victoria spoke with more certainty then speculation.

"What a wild theory. So why did a container land in the water?" Tola shook her head, watching Em step over a small shrub.

"Personally, I believe we have found a ship full of treasures. Just like those discovered by mining companies." Em's voice brimmed with enthusiasm. "Well, that's my theory."

Gratefully moving out of the sun's burning rays, the three entered the crevasse where they thought they had seen the metallic object.

"Are you sensing anything, Em?" Victoria said as she walked toward the flat unnatural surface. They stopped, standing shoulder to shoulder and looking at it.

"I do sense something, but it is not danger." Em nodded at Tola confidently, then looked to Victoria. "I am sure of it."

"Are you sure, Em?" Tola asked with a raised brow.

"I will check it out." Victoria moved to the dull metallic surface. "You two be ready with your weapons, just in case." She leaned forward and peered closely at it. "This is definitely a door of some kind. It seems to be covered by sediment."

"It also looks as if someone removed rocks that that were in front of it and threw them over there." Tola pointed to a pile of rocks just to the side.

"Yes, I just noticed that." Victoria frowned in puzzlement.

"That does not make any sense. Why would someone remove the rocks, and not enter?" Em said with some irritation.

A vivid memory came to Victoria's mind of the large illuminated hand that had lifted her supernaturally to safety. She let out a gasp that drew the other's attention. The vision vanished.

"What is it?" Em asked, with hands on her hips.

"It's nothing. I just find this exciting, that's all." Victoria pondered the vision in her spirit for a moment, contemplating why it would come to her now. Was there some connection to be made as to why her life had been spared and she'd been brought here to this Letalis moon? She looked carefully at the exposed surface and found a small oval impression to the right. "I believe this should open the door."

The other two took a step back, standing ready to respond to any danger. She swiped the thick dust off the panel with her left sleeve. A puff of the silt wafted up her nose and she lightly sneezed it out. Seeing a human hand's impression on the panel, she intuitively placed her palm on it. She immediately felt a strong tingling sensation. Uncertain of the meaning of that, she started to pull her hand away, but suddenly the panel began to glow, dimly at first, and then brighter.

"The access control must be able to charge itself with the electrical energy from my hand!" Her voice was filled with wonder.

She removed her hand and saw a green button at the top of the panel. She quickly pressed it. "Here we go," she said as the large door slid open. The hiss of pressurized stale air escaping washed over them.

"Looks like we are the first ones to open this door in a very long time." Victoria paused in the entrance, waiting for her eyes to adjust to the dark interior. Cautiously, Em and Tola came in on either side of her. The interior lighting flickered on.

"This is a ship of some kind, not a container module." Em's voice shook with excitement.

"Maybe this old ship just might have unclaimed treasure worth something!" Tola, still cautious, stepped farther in, pointing her weapon in every direction down the open hallway.

"Let's head directly to the bridge," Em suggested and moved to Tola's side.

"I agree, the bridge should give us a lot of information as to what type of vessel this is," Tola whispered, as if she would alert someone to their presence.

Victoria remained silent, reaching out with her spirit, searching for answers as to why she was here on this ship. Detecting life signatures, the ship's internal sensors activated using the remaining power from the energy cores. They breathed the newly recycled air, as they traversed several hundred meters along a main corridor, finally reaching the bridge section of the ship.

"Not bad for an old ship," Tola said admiringly. The sophisticated and beautifully designed interior had clearly been created by highly intelligent master builders. The three gazed around in amazement as they walked along a smooth corridor that curved upward to the main bridge.

"This design is similar to that used by the Mantis Alliance," Victoria commented, marveling at the ancient ship. The momentousness of this discovery was beginning to dawn on her.

"No…it's more similar to that used by the Krauvanok," Tola rebutted.

"How old do you suppose it is? I wonder what happened to the crew or passengers." Em's voice trailed off and she holstered her energy pistol.

"I have a sense that it is older than we would dare to believe, Em," Victoria said at her side.

"Look, over here!" Tola shouted, pointing to the raised portion of the bridge.

"This is most likely the command station," Em speculated as she examined one of the smaller stations on the platform's edge on her way to the command platform.

Tola adjusted herself on one of the large chairs, looking right at home as the hard-bitten mercenary she was. "I assume this is the captain's seat… This looks interesting, let's see what happens." Her right fingers brushed the dust off a series of lit alien symbols, and she pressed a flashing green tab in the center of the arm panel. A moment later an image appeared in front of them, three-dimensional and holographic, of a human male. They were amazed at how realistic it was. "Seems so real, good looking too…" Tola said, leaning forward with interest.

He began to speak but the language was unintelligible.

"What's he saying?"

"It sounds like the first language. You know, Reshmek?" Victoria voiced her thoughts aloud.

"Never heard of it." Em shrugged her shoulders, staring fixedly at the moving lips. Victoria walked over to the image and recited several passages of the holy Kodashah tome in Chavasug, a dialect of Reshmek, and then repeated it in common Tordesh. The image stopped speaking for a moment as if he were gathering his thoughts.

"Greetings, I am Captain Stephen Heedeth of the Ramah ambassadorial ship, Kirjath-Arba." The tall, dark-skinned image looked even more alive now.

Victoria examined the captain's uniform as he continued to speak. *This uniform was worn by the military of Ramah millennia ago!* She felt a strong sense of honor, as the ship bore the name of the city where she along with her family had lived. The recording continued explaining that they had crash-landed in a large lake after coming under attack from an unknown assailant. Apparently most had escaped in single shuttle pods, but a few had loyally remained behind to go down with ship. The captain pointed to a station near him, which lit up at his command. The lighting dimmed and then the holographic image vanished. The station that he had pointed to remained brightly lit.

"So, this is an ancient ambassador ship." Tola smiled with satisfaction. "Now I know why I've never seen one like it before.

This means they must have precious cargo on board, like you sensed, Em." She stood and made her way over to the lit station. She motioned for them to join her. "Let's see what the captain wanted us to find." Her voice was uncharacteristically eager with greed as she sat on a seat at the station and placed her hand on the panel.

Nothing happened.

"Hmm, not working." She got up from the seat and stood to the side. "Victoria, you're from Ramah, you should try." She waved her hand at the chair.

Wordlessly, the wayward sister sat down and placed her hand on a rectangular-shaped box and spoke in Tordesh. She was intensely grateful that the other two did not know what she was thinking, as a humbling wave flooded over her at the significance of this experience. "I am Victoria, of Ramah. I need access to the ship's logs."

A green light engulfed her hand and immediately the Reshmek symbols and letters on the display panel transformed to reflect its user's language. She cleared her throat, keeping her moistened eyes hidden.

"Nice, this should be a lot easier now." She remained seated and accessed the passenger and cargo manifests. "It looks like the ship was indeed carrying precious gemstones and other rare artifacts." Victoria felt intensely drawn to the passenger list.

"Yes, Em, did you hear that?! Precious stones and artifacts. We're rich!" Tola shouted with exuberant joy, all the while pumping her gloved fist in the air and jumping up and down.

"Someone must have found out about the precious cargo and attacked the ship," Em said with a frown.

"Let's go see if the cargo is still here. Victoria, can you locate where it was stored?" Tola rubbed her hands together in anticipation of the treasure hunt.

"Right here," she said quietly. A three-dimensional map appeared on the screen, showing their location relative to the cargo hold. Drawing a sharp, excited breath, Victoria spoke a name from the ship's list of personnel. "The ambassador was Sarai Chawah Modroya." She looked for the location of the sleeping quarters of the renowned woman.

"Who is she? I assume she was human. Am I right?" Tola's ignorance grated on her spirit.

"She was the wife of our great patriarch, Barabba Nobaveth Modroya, and is the matriarch of the tribes of Modroya," Victoria said, reverently.

"I suppose that you found yourself something of great value after all, Victoria." Tola's genuine smile did a lot to make up for her lack of knowledge.

"Why don't you go to her quarters and pay your respects, while we go to the cargo hold and look for treasure?" Em said. "We will come and get you when we're ready to leave." Her sincerity seemed to imply a level of trust for Victoria that had not been there previously.

"Thank you. I will wait for you at my matriarch's quarters." She shot up out of the seat and trotted off the bridge, breaking into a run just as soon as she was out of sight.

For a long stretch of time Victoria sat on the dusty floor near the foot of the bed, gazing at the deep purple sheet she had draped over the mummified remains of the founder of the Marium Kahnet, Sarai Chawah Modroya. Her soul was vexed with an overwhelming sense of her unworthiness of this precious discovery. The flood of memories of her unredeemable deeds had driven her to her knees.

She felt the warmth of tears dripping onto her hand as her head slumped in shame. She cupped her hand and caught several of them in her palm. *Please forgive me, Abba El.* A groaning deep in her spirit reached the surface and she wept softly for a moment, releasing some of the years of grief. "The return of Mother Sarai to Ramah will fulfill prophecy," she whispered in wonder. "Am I the one? Is this the reason you spared my life and brought me here?"

Rising from the dust-encrusted floor, she wiped the remnants of her tears with her sleeve and stood by Sarai's head. She had carefully placed the book of Yaqal, with newly written pages of the book of Yagahna, on top of it, by the Mother's enrobed body. She gently touched the pages with her index finger. "Am I to take you back to Ramah with me?" The vivid memories of her last moments as the Mecropex was destroyed struck her just then, and her entire body reacted shivering uncontrollably. "The Leviathans are alive somehow." The hairs on her arms rose along with the certainty of the knowledge that dropped into her spirit. The fierce and merciless races birthed within the dark wombs of evil struck great fear in her. Her stomach grumbled, but the desire to eat had left when she first stepped foot in the matriarch's quarters. She sensed that it was almost time to leave this tomb.

"Deliver the sacred scriptures to Ramah." A clear, deep male voice washed over her. Unnerved, she gasped and spun around, looking for the one who'd spoken, but found no one. "Deliver the sacred scriptures to Ramah," the voice repeated the command.

"I will do as I am asked." Her voice quavered, as this had never happened to her before.

"As written in the book of Yaqal, her bones will rest in Ramah. You will keep this in her heart and in the time appointed as Abba El promised her, Sarai's bones will lie where she was born." His voice filled with the immense power of Bayit El echoed in the room. Silence once again descended, but it was now filled with purpose and promise.

Victoria finally dared to lift her head. "They're gone… Now I know for certain why I was spared. I have a part in fulling prophecy. But I don't understand—why me? Look at what I did! I killed so many innocent people." Victoria remained on the floor, perplexed and joyful. Self-condemnation fled away.

Then a strong sense that whoever had attacked the ship was not interested in the cargo, but the ambassador herself, came into her mind. She heard footsteps approaching from deep within the bowels of the ship. She carefully picked up the ancient tomes.

"I make an oath to you, Mother Sarai. I will return these sacred texts back to Ramah. With Abba El's help you will be brought back home too." Holding them tight to her torso, she turned and saw the smudged faces of Em and Tola at the entrance to the quarters.

"We have relocated the cargo to a secret location." Tola's strangely disconnected tone jarred the somewhat reverent atmosphere in the room.

"Are you ready to go?" she said in a quieter tone, seeing the small body on the bunk in the spare but elegant quarters.

Em looked with interest at the old books Victoria held protectively to her chest. "Is this her?" she asked, staring at the draped remains.

"This is the founder of the Marium Kahnet, Sarai Chawah Modroya," Victoria said quietly, swallowing a fresh lump in her throat.

"Say your goodbyes to her, Victoria." Tola's tone was not unkind, but it was clear she was uncomfortable. She nodded at Victoria with understanding, then said more firmly, "Ok then, let's get going. Raduu could return at any time. It's best if he finds us where he left us." She placed her dusty gloves on her hips. Victoria looked at the Mother Sarai once more.

"Come on, let's go, Victoria." Em gestured for Victoria to precede her.

It was a relief to leave the scene of the demise of so many. Even after all of this time, the sprawled remains of the crew were a grim reminder of the great price that had been paid to protect Mother Sarai. Victoria breathed deeply, feeling a sense of hope. The sun was setting and they hastily made their way back to the safety of the plateau before the creatures of the night emerged.

Chapter Five

LETALIS

Nia and Taona gazed out at the horizon through the viewport of a modified military grade personnel transport, admiring the pristine snowcapped Shebar Mountains, as they flew to their destination. "Do you still believe that our arrangements to get the ship we need are assured?" Nia asked. She pressed her lips together, noting Taona's set expression.

"You know we had no choice but to accept Dukar Gruppa's offer... We help him get what he needs and we get a ship. We have his word as a Muak'Xod Dukar." Taona's words did not seem too convincing.

"Of course I know that, but that doesn't mean this is a good decision. What good is that deal if we die of radiation poisoning?" Her eyebrows lifted, emphasizing her point.

"I want to remind you that we took the only opportunity we had in order to get our hands on a ship capable of traveling long distances with radiation protection too," Taona stated in her usual pragmatic way. "It will get us to the Letalis moon, but ultimately back home to Ramah."

Nia frowned deeply, still concerned about their safety. Traveling directly into the path of a large swathe of Cremindraux radiation was not a wise decision.

The ship's control panels lit up with a bevy of flashing lights, accompanied by a succession of audible warnings.

"Data shows we have entered a pocket of Cremindraux radiation." Taona's calm voice and stoic demeanor was one of many facets of her character that had been shaped by her training as a young Marium Kahnet disciple. "Our ship's gravity dampening generator is offline." Her fingers flew across the main control panel, compensating for the sporadic energy losses in the various ship systems.

"I am deactivating external protective plating, it is offline," Nia shouted over the loud alarms. "Diverting power to the gravity auxiliary cores."

Taona deactivated the auto assist navigation system and external sensors. "Too much interference from the radiation. I'm going to have to take us in manually." Taona's confidence was reassuring. The ship seemed to level out for the time being.

Nia felt a slight burn in her throat and swallowed to relieve the irritation. It seemed to be getting worse, so she knew she needed some help. Coming to a quick decision, she pulled out her last Cymbratar gel tab. She looked closely at it, noting the once red oblong gel tab had turned a darker hue. The mysterious properties that made it sparkle in sparse light had been altered. Now ripples of iridescent blues washed over its surface.

"Look!" Nia shoved the tab in front of Taona's face.

"What?" Taona said, annoyed. "Forget about it for now." She shook her head, dismissively, then gently pushed Nia's hand away from her face.

Nia pressed the surface of the tab with her finger and was not surprised to find that it was slightly harder than it had been before. She shrugged her shoulders and popped it into her mouth.

"Wait—don't!" Taona's hand darted to intercept hers, but it was too late. "Nia, what were you thinking?!" She slapped her open palm on her armrest.

"I don't know why I did that." Fear sliced through Nia's veins, then suddenly her body went rigid. A single sharp point of acute pain shot through her temples. *Yes, that was a very bad idea.* She clenched her teeth. She tasted death on her tongue and began trying to spit out its metallic bitterness. Her body began to quiver with a strong chill sliding up and down her body. *I am going to die.* The single thought froze in her mind.

"Are you alright?" Taona placed her hand on Nia's shaking shoulder.

"No, I feel sick to my stomach and a bit cold." Her teeth began to chatter loudly. "Aren't you?" Her worried gaze met Taona's.

"Yes, the internal climate control systems are offline." Taona broke off and quickly made power distribution adjustments to warm the cabin, then turned back to help Nia. "Turn this way, I need to see something. Your skin looks slightly discolored." Taona's mouth snapped shut and she frowned. "It must be the effects from the altered Cymbratar."

Nia's thoughts drifted to her family on Ramah. *I will see you soon.* She had a sense she would die very soon.

"Nia hang in there, you'll be alright." She instantly felt hope rise at Taona's encouraging words. "We knew this was not going to be as easy as Dukar Gruppa made it out to be," Taona said, changing the subject.

It was quiet for a moment while the ship skimmed along the northernmost tip of the Shebar Mountains, nearly to their destination. Feeling marginally better, Nia peered through the canopy, looking at thick funnels of smoke from crash sites in the distance.

"I still believe that we should send a coded message to Fay. You know she is waiting for us." She gazed at Taona, waiting for her usual emotionless response.

"We have gone over this many times. By now we have been reported as missing and are most likely prime suspects in the destruction of the Stadageo." Taona's face had a look of empathy.

It would be a huge emotional burden if Fay were caught because she was waiting for them. Nia's eyes welled with tears that she was trying to hold back.

"Look I understand, but we have to follow our plans. Fay is most likely in an Ausertane safe house. That is what I would have done if we were late." Taona nodded, emphasizing her point. She kept darting glances at Nia. "Don't worry," she said, and gently patted Nia's left hand reassuringly. "Remember, we told Fay not to wait too long before leaving the secondary meeting place. Then, if necessary go by herself back to Ramah with the information we have gathered.

The Mantis Alliance must know what has happened here. Besides, she is more likely to be concerned about us not showing up." She smiled as Nia nodded, then adjusted her headgear on her lap. "You look better Nia, now let's get this ship landed."

Taona expertly maneuvered the transport between treacherous outcroppings of splintered rocks down the slopes of Shebar Mountain. Through the transparent canopy of the sleek transport, they could see Perrapenta about sixty kilometers distant. Sadness loomed over them with the knowledge that Perrapenta, a previously busy metropolis, was now a mass gravesite for millions of sentient beings.

"Do you remember where we are to land?" Taona asked, surveying the landscape for the telltale landmark.

"Yes." Nia recalled the diagrams and map of their destination with such clarity and detail it was if she were viewing them on a live holographic display. "I see it!" She pointed slightly to the right with her gloved finger. "Ten degrees starboard, about three thousand meters, just past the piles of scrap." Nia was surprised by the vast improvement of her vision.

"You can see that from here?" Taona stared at her quizzically.

"Must be the effects of the transformed Cymbratar." Nia swallowed hard. "I feel sick to my stomach." She winced in discomfort.

"Don't worry, once we return to Ramah, I am sure that the elders will help us." Taona slowed the transport, and they hovered momentarily.

"Do you really think they will be able to help get the Cymbratar out of our bodies?" Nia's voice held a note of hope.

"Yes, out of both of us. But for now, I need you to focus on our mission." Taona's voice held an edge. She leaned forward and re-entered the landing sequence.

"Landing systems are offline." The ship's automated, monotone voice echoed in the small craft.

Taona placed her gloved hands over the main control panel. "This is not going to be easy." She shook her head, and prepared to land manually.

"Is there any aspect of this mission that will go smoothly?" Nia couldn't help her outburst of frustration.

"Hold on!" Their bodies jerked violently as the ship hit the hard frozen snow, it skidded a bit, then groaned to a halt. It sounded unnaturally loud to Nia. "We made it," Taona said victoriously.

It seemed a hollow victory to Nia in light of the hardship still ahead. As if in slow motion, they geared up for the harsh weather outside and without another word stepped out of the cockpit.

"Finally." Nia's speech created a small white cloud as her warm breath met the harsh Letalis winter's air. A sense of relief washed over her as they successfully made makeshift repairs to the cargo door control pad, allowing the thick metal door to operate properly.

"We better activate our face shields and our communications link.

My face is starting to freeze." A large, white bilious cloud moved over Nia's her face.

"How are you feeling?" Taona asked, somewhat tentatively. Nia noticed her staring fixedly at her face with a glowering frown.

Nia laughed, then stretched her hands upwards and bent herself backwards. She twisted her upper torso from side to side. "I feel great! Now turn around and let me check your auxiliary energy pack." She inspected Taona's clothing as she turned completely around. "Looks good to me, now check mine." Nia quickly spun around.

"Turn around once more and not so fast." Nia rolled her eyes and turned around again more slowly. "Looks good." Taona moved her arms around in a wide circular motion. "I am very sore. It feels like those safety straps cut into my bones. And no, I am not taking any of those contaminated Cymbratar gel tabs." Her firm tone made it clear that she was adamant about her decision.

They both carefully inspected and activated the power cores of their MX 9 energy pistols favored by Muak'Xod agents. The pistols were some of the largest and most powerful handheld weapons available.

"How about that... they actually work. It's about time something on this mission goes our way!" Nia's beaming smile was designed to reassure Taona, who seemed to be overly concerned about her physical and maybe even mental capacity to carry out the mission.

"Okay, let's go," Taona said in a doubtful tone.

With their pistols drawn, they opened the cargo door and leapt out of the ship, landing firmly on an exposed rock surface a meter below. They navigated around the snow-covered piles of antiquated equipment. In the distance loomed storm clouds that carried with them the deathly rain of Cremindraux radiation. They had to retrieve the mysterious object described by Dukar Gruppa and leave before the area was blanketed with those clouds of death.

Nia turned and noticed that Taona had slowed a bit, trudging through the snow, and the distance between them was increasing. "We have to move faster," Nia shouted into her communications link. It was clear that Taona was pushing herself to keep up. Nia was relieved to see her clear the last snow-covered obstacle. Now there only a hundred meters of a cleared path stood between them and their destination.

Halfway to the partially hidden entrance, Nia suddenly felt a presence and a horrible sensation of dread wash over her, and she slowed. "Look, over there, coming this way." Nia's voice rang clearly in Taona's headgear. She looked to where Nia was pointing.

Groups of black, elongated spheres of various sizes were gliding just above the snow-covered ground. Even in the morning light, waves of blue iridescence were visible radiating around them.

"What are those?" asked Nia.

"I'm not sure, but they seem to be heading in this general direction." Taona pointed her weapon at the strange objects, and Nia touched the protective visor of her headgear.

"Taona, I feel something strange on my forehead. Do you see anything?" Her voice sounded strained.

"I see a strange black mark in the center of your forehead." Taona paused, then said softly, "It appeared after you took the altered Cymbratar." She turned to look at the spheres.

"You saw it back on the ship and you said nothing?" Nia's face flushed with anger. "Why didn't you say anything?!"

"I didn't want to worry you. I asked you how you felt and you said you felt fine after you warmed up." Taona silently pointed at a few of the spheres, which had changed course and were most definitely headed their way. "We better hurry. We can still make it to the entrance well before those things come too close to us." She turned and jogged to the entrance of the building. Just to be sure, they kept their pistols trained on the menacing spheres that were coming ever closer.

"I think it's best if you keep your eyes on those objects." She nudged Nia's shoulder. "Here, use this." She handed over her weapon. Nia grabbed it and aimed at the approaching objects with both weapons.

"There are five of them about six hundred meters away headed right for us." By the lack of her sister's response, Nia could tell that their communication link was breaking up.

At the entrance, Taona found an access panel and entered the code Dukar Gruppa had given them. "I got it!" The tall, narrow door slid open and she retrieved her weapon. Quickly, they entered a long chamber, crouched and ready to defend themselves. Hearing the door slide shut behind them, they relaxed marginally.

The ceiling was a large, shallow dome. Its dim lighting seemed intentional, giving the place an atmosphere of clandestine missions conducted in the shadows. In the center was a cluster of strange machines similar to those used within the Stadageo. At the bottom of the ramp, they stopped to marvel at the beautiful colorful display of energy, which surged through the various semi-transparent components atop the group of miniature Necronos-like pods.

"We better hurry, and find what we came for." Nia's words seemed to be absorbed into the dense walls.

"Yes, those things will be here shortly. I doubt that metal door will prevent their entrance." Taona moved with renewed urgency as they rounded a corner and found five bodies lying on the ground a few meters away from the main machine.

Nia walked up to the deceased, bent over, and examined one of the larger alien individuals. "This one has a signet ring given to Krauvanok Alliance Overseers. He also has the mark of a Kravjin elder on his left hand." She frowned.

"This one is a female Etrakkian." Taona's statement was garbled, but Nia recognized the thin-bodied alien and nodded in acknowledgement. Taona quickly moved around each corpse, examining their uniforms. "Most are wearing Synogog clothing. These two have bioengineering insignias. What are they doing here?" Nia could tell Taona was baffled, as they did not have any obvious wounds either.

She tapped Taona's shoulder. "Maybe they were working on that." She pointed with her MX 9 energy pistol to a fantastically beautiful box. "Dukar Gruppa said we would know what it was when we saw it." Her voice held a note of excitement.

But just as they took a single step toward it, a fearful presence overshadowed them. It was a familiar one that they had sensed before. On guard, Nia pointed to their far right. The same oblong onyx object that they'd seen outside entered the chamber through the wall. She tapped Taona's arm with her elbow, silently drawing her attention to the last of the strange pulsating ovate objects that had just emerged through the wall. The five objects moved toward the bodies of the deceased. The waves of blue iridescence had increased in speed, causing a strobe effect. Without a word, with their fingers twitching on the triggers, they backed away from the five corpses in unison.

Shimmering waves of blue shifted upward as each hovered above the heads of the deceased. Taona nudged Nia and pointed with her weapon to their prize cradled between two dragon-shaped devices, about a meter and a half above the floor. Nia nodded in acknowledgement but remained standing still, enraptured by the events unfolding in front of them.

Just then, fine golden sparkling mist emerged from the torsos of the five individuals as they were drawn and absorbed into the bottoms of the five pulsating devices. Nia knew that Taona, like herself, was struggling in her spirit to comprehend what was transpiring right in front of them. The golden mist cleared but was immediately replaced with a dark mist in which Nia thought she saw the faces of the deceased drawn into the onyx intruders. A moment later, they sensed that the objects were living organisms of some sort, and were now focused on them. They both tightened their grip on their weapons, prepared to fire.

One of the objects glided toward them and stopped two meters away from Nia. A small cloud of sparkling crystalline mist emerged from the top of the sphere. Nia stared at the horrified look on Taona's face, but was helpless to do anything. *Why isn't she shooting?* Nia felt her body seize as the mist reached her, and then she began to shudder.

"It hurts, Taona—I feel heat on my forehead and a lot of pain. Please do something."

Nia's harsh, whispered plea jolted Taona into action. Taona pointed her pistol at the sphere.

"You will not fire your weapon." The strong, commanding voice echoed very loudly around them.

Taona turned completely around with back and forth sweeping motions, seeking who had spoken to her. But she saw no one.

The sound of Nia's weapon clattering to the ground drew Taona's attention back to her. Her arms hung limply at her sides, then she collapsed to the floor. The mist vanished, and the mysterious entity moved away from them to re-join the others. They all disappeared through the walls.

Taona ran to Nia, knelt down, and was relieved to see that she was breathing. "You're still alive." She almost teared up with joy. Realizing that she needed to complete the mission, she stood and stared at the strange machine. Faces of humanoids and other alien beings were depicted on its surface. All the faces were frozen in grimaces of terror. One of them reminded her of the Kravjin lying dead in the room.

A fiery sensation in her Cymbratar-modified cells began to race through her veins in reaction to an unseen force. She felt a drip from her nose that she licked from her lip. It was blood and the metallic flavor caused her neck and head to tingle. A strange sense of distance from reality enfolded her and in her mind's eye, a transparent being appeared in front of her. It hovered momentarily, then took the form of a statuesque human woman.

The regal-looking woman was in a state of divine serenity, enveloped by a strange glow. On her head was a golden crown and five stars hovered above her. Shadowy mist-like beings floated on either side of her. "You will take the broaches from Priestess Tmexa, and bring it to me along with samples of what is contained within the emerald box at that machine. After which you will be taken to a place of your choosing." Her words held great authority. It was clear she was very powerful.

Taona looked left and right as five more female forms took shape around her. They all wore similar religious robes to the woman. Her curiosity was irrevocably piqued. She felt compelled to find out more about this religion that she had never seen or heard of before, and more importantly a way of escape off Letalis.

"I am honored to be chosen for this task." Taona's voice held a note of awe she could not hide.

"You are to come alone. You will take one of the transports near this chamber and leave immediately. Do not fail us, or you will die." The divine lady's face began to glow even more brightly.

"I want to be able to take two companions with me to the place of my choosing," Taona felt emboldened to say, with the realization these ethereal women needed her help.

A pause ensued, then the glow enveloped Taona and a sense of danger pricked at her spirit. "Let it be as you have said. But if you fail me, you will die...come alone!" The lady's voice trailed off, and a moment later she and her entourage vanished.

Taona snapped out of the trance and quickly regained her bearings. She found herself standing right next to the ornate metallic box. Replaying the strange women's request and warning, she noticed Nia getting up off the floor. Taona holstered her weapon and came to her side. "Nia, are you alright?" she asked with genuine concern.

"Yes, I think so. My head aches terribly but my nose has stopped bleeding. Are they gone?" Nia asked, looking around the room.

Taona looked at her sharply, then realized she was referring to the strange objects. "Yes, they are gone."

"Then let's get out of here."

They retracted their face shields to get a better look at the maroon and grey box. "I will hold onto these two corners. Ready?" Nia's hot breath created a billow of white mist.

"Yes," Taona said, grasping her side of the box.

"On 3... 1, 2, 3." Nia grunted as they lifted the heavy box. It was so heavy, they lost their grip on it and it crashed to the floor.

Taona sucked in a breath. "Let's hope what's inside isn't damaged," she exclaimed, bending down to examine it further. Nia knelt on the other side and placed her hand on it.

"Let's remove the lid and find out what Dukar Gruppa wants."
She acknowledged Taona's nod of agreement. "Now."

They both grunted as they lifted the heavy lid off. The clanking
of the metal hitting the floor echoed in the chamber. A small white
book with a strange symbol in the center of its cover lay inside,
along with an emerald box and stacks of red pentagon-shaped
wafers. Taona reached in and picked up some of the wafers with
her gloved hands. They were surprisingly heavy, and some fell to the
ground. Looking at one of them closely, she saw a raised center with
an unrecognizable symbol on it, like the book.

"They probably ate these and died," Nia remarked as she placed
the wafers in a compartment in her utility belt.

Taona retrieved a data pad near the containment box lid. "Look
what I found—wait, it's too cold." She activated her face visor, as
did Nia. "It's still on… Listen to this. According to the notes in the
log, they were developing a process to modify and refine Cymbratar
into a substance they call Nembratar. The data indicates it will have
the ability to prolong one's life for hundreds of years."

Nia wore a look of marvel, mixed with skepticism, on her face.
"Now we know why Dukar Gruppa wants this box." Taona pieced
together Nia's garbled words, as the communication devices in their
helmets were still not operating correctly.

Taona continued to read the log. After a few moments, she spoke
in a somewhat distracted tone. "These symbols and equations are
very similar to the Nostrohelix used in the Stadageo. The last entry

has the ancient symbol for the Zhanifra galaxy, followed by a long sequence of Toxrokk numbers, then symbols for the Malgavatta and Kilodromus galaxies. But they do not have a sequence of numbers associated with them." Taona deactivated the data pad and placed it in the emerald box.

"I believe this could be just one of several locations where they are working on this new substance," she said in a distracted tone, but with some certainty that she was right. Her thoughts turned to the dire warning she had received just moments before and her spirit quailed in her belly. Feeling impending danger, she sprang into action, grabbing the rest of the wafers. "Here, put these into the emerald box. These are what Dukar Gruppa wanted, and don't forget this white book." She stood up and watched Nia place the items in the pockets of her winter clothing, then get to her feet with the emerald box in her hand.

"Are you ready to leave this morbid place? I sure am," Nia said as she turned to leave. Taona did not move. Nia stopped and frowned at her. "What is it, is there something wrong? Taona, you seem far away! We need to hurry." Her voice held anxiety and concern.

"I don't have time to explain, but I will later. I must go to a certain place not far from here. I have been told to go alone," Taona said, adamantly. She placed her hands on Nia's shoulders, her visor bumping Nia's. "You will have to return without me. Give Dukar Gruppa that box and explain what happened here. Tell him that I had to attend to a personal matter and we are to meet in the capital of Kramatau. I believe that I will be contacting you with some good news." She smiled reassuringly.

"What are you talking about?" Nia shook her head. "We always do things together! I think the oath we spoke just days ago should mean something." Her tone was a bit petulant, and moisture welled in her eyes. "Who told you to do what?"

"You were passed out on the floor and as I was making my way over to help you when a woman wearing religious vestments appeared. I was instructed to deliver certain items to a specific place right now. I was told to go alone or there would be dire repercussions. She promised that after I deliver what she requests that all of us will be taken to any place we desired. I agreed just in case Dukar Gruppa can't deliver on his promise. Nia, it doubles our chances of escaping. Remember the oath we took years ago? Damage the Stadageo, then return home to Ramah and rebuild our lives in honor of our families no matter the risk. To be honest with you, after all this time that has passed, my heart burns with a strong desire to return home in a way that I have not experienced since I first left seeking revenge. What about you?" Taona waited calmly to see if Nia was convinced.

"Yes, I feel the same, but this sounds extremely risky." Nia frowned, clearly worried.

"Don't worry, it's a simple enough task. You must trust me, my dear friend!" Her tone blocked the argument she knew was coming.

"I don't understand. A strange women appeared to you and asked you to do something." Nia shook her head again. "I don't think I can do this alone," she admitted.

"You are not coming with me. The woman clearly warned me to come by myself. It seemed to me that she is not one to be trifled with." Taona replied firmly.

"I don't fully understand, or agree with you sis, but let it be as you wish… I trust you." Nia moved to hug her, squeezing her briefly.

"I won't leave this place until I see your ship leave," Taona said and pressed her lips together, waiting for Nia to meet her gaze. "I give you my word. I will explain everything when we are reunited once again." Her sincerity appeared to soothe her friend's troubled heart, and she relaxed a bit.

"How are you going to get there if I'm taking our ship?" Nia cocked her head to the side with a look of curiosity on her face.

"Well… I was told that these poor soulless individuals lying here arrived in transports that are hidden somewhere nearby." She placed her hands on her hips with an air of mild impatience.

Nia sighed and appeared to relent. "Very well, I will see you soon then." She turned and strode past the machines.

Taona trailed slightly behind her, stopping at the doorway. She stood silent, until moments later she saw the small energy signatures of the ship disappear in the distance heading back to Dukar Gruppa. Noticing the dark storm clouds approaching in the night sky, she sprang into action.

Chapter Six

TARTARUS

Staring in the direction of the Mecropex through the viewport in his quarters, Gandu Khanon felt the pull of the vortex. "I must redeem myself. There must be a way to enter it." He would ask his master, Abaddon, if it were possible.

As he had done many times before, he easily transitioned into a transcendental state. Effortlessly, he glided through a thick grey mist. Unintelligible whispers swirled around him and words written within the book of Eronash, the path of dark powers, echoed loudly in every direction. Three Creminmorta covenant symbols appeared in front of him, moving closer and closer. One was made of blood, the second of gold, and the third was a Daugravog stone. He passed through them in succession. As he did, their raw, intoxicating power energized his flesh and spirit. Looking down for a moment, he saw the crimson sea. Multitudes of whirlpools appeared in its dark depths. He heard the cries and screams of the souls from the five realms of Creminmorta that ascended up to the throne of the Tisrad Dragon. He felt callous to their plight. *They deserved it, I am sure.*

Suddenly, he found himself standing atop a large hill, surrounded by ancient Audramore trees. A stone altar rose up from a mound in the center of the dusty barren surface, just several short meters in front of him. Twelve winged serpent beings emanating sulfurous curls of smoke all around descended like striking predators on either side of the rubescent oblong stone altar. The ominous serpent apparitions reformed themselves into humanoid forms. The tall, powerful beings were cloaked in ceremonial robes and stood motionless. He suddenly recognized something was different on this transcendental journey. It was a rarely performed ritual and he swelled with pride, silently marveling. *The ceremony of Galgothom.*

"There should be thirteen participants. I only see twelve." Just as he muttered the words his body was picked up and thrust to the side of the altar. He knew better than to struggle. The hoods of the robes hid the others' identities from him, but he looked from one face to the other, trying to discover who they were. They were also separated from him behind shields of nebula energy. He glanced at his own garments and was not surprised that he too wore similar ceremonial robes. *I am the thirteenth priest...* He looked at his Nazar signet ring, then noticed his family crest on the edge of the oblong alter. There were other family crests that he did not recognize.

A wave of cold descended upon him and he felt a strong presence above him. He looked straight up into the single eye of the Tisrad Dragon. Inside of the eye were countless religious symbols. He immediately knew that it was Navmolek; god of religion, one of the five spirits of the Tisrad Dragon, called Spirradeus.

"With the Ruaphesh blade, you will make a holy sacrifice to me," a voice from the eye spoke loudly. The power of it shook his bones.

In that instant, a weighty object appeared in Khanon's right hand. He clutched it—it was a holy blade that had been forged in the lake of sacred blood, deep in the realm of Hemosongra. As he marveled at its dark beauty, it came alive and began to speak. *It sounds like Toxrokk, but I can't make out the words.* The mysterious language was used in the five realms of Creminmorta. He sensed the blade's overwhelming thirst for blood.

Just then, a small human male child appeared on the altar. His young flesh was olive, his tiny head thick with dark, silky hair. His eyes were tightly shut, and tears were streaming down his plump cheeks. *Strange, I can't hear him.* Khanon distantly considered the soundless phenomena, then sharply looked at the holy blade of Ruaphesh that was writhing in his hand.

His spirit moved unencumbered, as if he had performed this blood offering ceremony many times before. Gripping the living instrument with both hands, he plunged the blade into the sacrifice with all of his might. Feeling the warmth of the blood shoot up onto his hands, he saw the child's face become his own. Gasping, Khanon released his grip, and felt the dagger in his heart.

Suddenly out of the trance, he leaned his forehead on the viewport in front of his face. "What just happened?" he said with both anger and fear causing him to break out in a sweat. He placed both hands on his chest, breathing heavily. He could feel the pain slowly subsiding and wiped the sweat from his brow.

"Now approaching Tartarus," a monotone announcement rang throughout the ship.

With a grunt, he stretched his arms upwards, shaking off the experience. He reached into his vestment, retrieved the remaining portion of Cymbratar, and swallowed it. Shaking his head, he moved with purpose to his workstation, where a green beacon was urgently flashing on the display screen. Khanon quickly gathered his thoughts, then opened communications. The familiar face appeared of his protégé, Adad Mahath, one of the youngest among the humanoids to ascend to the rank of Qwravasha high priest.

"Lord Khanon, greetings," the red-skinned Akateco said in his customary gritty voice. The Akateco were known for their innate understanding of the ways of the holy book of Eronash. "We have confirmed reports, as you well know, that the Mecropex is in a multiphasic vortex, causing the Pratheous moon to fracture into large pieces." He paused for a moment, then continued, "We have also confirmed that the Stadageos on Letalis and Necropis have also been completely destroyed, releasing vast amounts of Cremindraux radiation… The initial reports are in that there are millions of casualties on both planets." He waited, expressionless.

Khanon's chest expanded as his lungs filled with cold air. He was unmoved by the loss of life. "I will meet you at the temple, as soon as I arrive." His mind began to strategize how to make the best of his circumstances.

"Very well, Lord Khanon…be protected by the Tisrad Dragon." Akateco bowed, then repeated the blessing. "Mullgoth."

Khanon responded in kind before ending communications. The piercing sound of an incoming message from the bridge came, and his nostrils flared. He leaned into the screen atop a desk.

"Lord Khanon, this is Captain Falco. We are entering the orbit of Tartarus. There is a priority one message on the bridge for you."

Khanon stretched his shoulders back and stared at his Nazar signet ring, barely acknowledging Falco. "Very well. I am on my way and I do not need an escort." His soul stirred with anger, mourning the loss of his project.

"As you wish, Lord Khanon." Captain Falco nodded, then the screen went blank.

With all of the setbacks he had suffered, he reached out for comfort. Not too long ago, he had learned a new way of communication with the Kravjin council called the Gurasaud, which gave him the ability to transport his spirit body to another location. With his eyes closed, he began to meditate and focus on the mother of his children and possessor of his heart since his youth. Although he was more advanced and gifted than his peers, he had yet to reach the full state of Gurasaud. Adding to the difficulty was the interference of multiphasic energies caused by the destruction of the Mecropex complex. Nonetheless, using the soul ties between himself and his wife, he would be able to send part of his spirit home.

Across the shimmering starburst bridge that spanned a great distance, he saw his wife Adramina reach up with both hands into a thick-leaved branch that shook as she plucked its ripe offering. Her pleased smile warmed his heart. He watched, comforted, as she raised the fruit to smell it. The plump, dark red and purple Pomevethia she held in her delicate hands was their favorite early summer fruit. He could sense that her spirit was stirred; she whispered in Toxrokk. Then, a moment later, he found himself in her hands. Her eyes sparkled like jewels at him.

"You are home," she said in a hushed tone, puckered her lips, and kissed the fruit.

Before he could respond, his spirit was thrust out of the visitation. He felt a trickle of liquid from his nose pool on his upper lip and smelled the distinct odor of his Cymbratar-infused blood.

"How much longer will it take for us to create a superior alternative?" he yelled loudly and wiped the drop off of his lip.

The ship-wide announcement that the Prakus had reached Tartarus orbit sounded. He turned and left his quarters, heading for the bridge.

Khanon called forth his necronos power and exited the transpod, onto the main bridge, in full stride. Every step sparked with the power of Necronecromic energy. He sensed the occasional gazes of those manning various battle stations, as they became aware of the ancient cold presence as he passed. A hundred meters ahead on the distinctive primary battle command platform stood security guards. Just beyond them were the Prakus' senior military leaders and Captain Falco. Peering out the battle bridge viewport, Khanon saw dozens of Varkrato league military ships silhouetted against the haunting violet and deep emerald moon of Tartarus. The ships were dwarfed by the seventeen thousand meter long Krauvanok Negury class super battle cruiser in their midst. In the distance, the multiphasic vortex was causing havoc on every ship. He felt the waves of fear and anxiety in the atmosphere as the senior command staff struggled to maintain control over the power core regulators and other critical systems. They could only hope the intensity of the multiphasic energy waves hitting them would begin to decrease.

"Lord Khanon." Captain Falco's emotionless tone was cursory. He immediately turned back to the task at hand. "Security clearance level one," he spoke clearly into the wide holographic screen in front of him. A beam of green light scanned Falco's forehead. A luminescent duplicate of his DNA was retrieved and flashed briefly on the screen.

Khanon stepped to the side of the captain and read the words that appeared: Authorization Granted. He remained motionless, but his spirit jerked back at the unexpected, sudden appearance of the Kravjin supreme leader, Chi Ku Ren, before them. A malevolent presence loomed over them, as they watched arcing thin threads of blue and red energy discharge from Ren's garments.

"Lord Khanon, once you arrive at Kurjafa, you will board a waiting transport ship that will bring you directly here." The solemn expression on the supreme leader's face did not bode well.

"Yes, your excellency, as you command." Khanon nodded his head respectfully, then ended the communication.

Anticipating Khanon's next request, Captain Falco said, "Lord Khanon, you may use the Matter Transportation Portal near the bridge to transport to the surface." Another section of the display screen began to display rapidly scrolling data. "The MTP's functionality will not be affected by the vortex waves, so it is safe to use." His voice was full of unwavering confidence.

"Very well then, Captain Falco." Khanon's rumbling stomach

reminded him that he had not eaten for a long time. He was pleased that his Kravjin clothing muffled its sound. Sensing the approach of someone, they turned to see Thygan Kruel. The insignia of Grand Inquisitor on the distinctively designed uniform of the high-ranking KMI officer glistened in the lighting. Kruel had a very large sphere of influence and as such was no one to be trifled with.

"Lord Khanon, I understand you are leaving for Kurjafa shortly. I wanted to personally inform you that Commander Mindendra's assignment to your project has expired." His piercing solid black eyes were filled with unspoken mistrust. "Since she has served with distinction during these most perilous events, my superiors have wisely reassigned her to the Regional Inquisitors office in Kurjafa. The commander has been promoted to the rank of Praetor Inquisitor." His declarations seethed with clandestine motives.

Khanon's eyebrows rose slightly as he pondered the change. *This will make entering more secure locations much easier.* "Inform your superiors that I am pleased with their decision that Praetor Inquisitor Mindendra has been re-assigned to my home planet." His stomach growled loudly.

"I suggest you take the time to have a meal and refresh yourself, Lord Khanon." Kruel's mild smug tone made his ridicule clear.

"In due time, Grand Inquisitor." His tone was dismissive and was clearly intended to put Kruel in his place.

"Shall we proceed, Lord Khanon?" asked the captain.

"After you." Khanon motioned with his right hand.

Captain Falco headed along a narrow pathway toward the MTP.

Many thoughts went through Khanon's mind as he left the command platform. *How did the Grand Inquisitor know so quickly that I had been summoned to Kurjafa? Does the KMI utilize some of the techniques that we do? Or is it something else altogether? It's apparent that the KMI don't trust me. Clever, using someone I trust. That is something I would do.* He laughed inside.

"Deactivate shielding," Captain Falco spoke as soon as they stepped onto the raised metal portion of the MTP portal equipment, just past the guard detail. A semi-golden transparent wall vanished, allowing access to the main MTP platform. Khanon stepped onto the raised surface in the center that could easily accommodate half a dozen soldiers. Captain Falco moved his hands within a three-dimensional holographic screen. "Activating matter transmission."

Those were the last words Khanon heard before he re-materialized just outside the temple grounds of Kurjafa.

As expected, there were only the temple Vothombot sentries. They immediately scanned him. "Welcome, Lord Khanon. Your transportation is waiting for you at the bottom of the ramp," the sentry said in its automaton, metallic voice.

As Khanon stepped toward the waiting transport, he became aware of the dense humid air on his face. He was glad that the Kravjin head covering absorbed the beads of sweat that ran along his temples. Although he enjoyed every Tartarian season, the transition into summer was the most uncomfortable for him. He looked at the dark shadows on the ground caused by clusters of low bluish clouds moving westward, as he strode down the ramp. A half a kilometer away was another MTP platform used exclusively by those traveling to and from the Augrasaur. As with all Kravjin temples located throughout the Quintástraya, entry restrictions were stickily adhered to. He sat on the edge of his seat after boarding the small transport that was taking him to the Kravjin temple. A moment later he was on his way along the mountainside slopes.

Khanon peered deeply into the forest below and with his extrasensory abilities he detected the presence of a large alpha predator crouching, preparing to pounce on unsuspecting prey. It was just one of many that inhabited the dense and ancient forests of Tartarus. He grinned with pleasure that some hapless prey was about to meet its bloody end.

Just ahead the dense shroud of mist was lifting, revealing several prominent tanzanite crystalline obelisks jutting into the midday sky. The transport glided closely by a row of golden ziggurats that were placed in specific locations throughout the bronze-plated surface of the grand and majestic Augrasaur temple grounds. The sight never failed to inspire him and his chest swelled with pride.

The transport slowed as they passed several other temple buildings, signaling they were about to land. Khanon spoke Toxrokk-empowered pronouncements of favor and protection, which echoed within the otherwise empty ship. The words encouraged him and he calmly gathered his thoughts.

"Lord Khanon, you have arrived at the gates of Houssadoom," said an ethereal voice that appeared to come from all around him.

Quickly exiting the transport now at a standstill, he was pleased with the cooler, less humid air around the main temple. On the pathway over the bridge ahead were two large dragons whose upper torsos extended out from the temple walls at the main temple gates. Their wings cast a large shadow and their fierce appearance made them seem life-like. Boldly striding over the bridge, he noticed far below in murky waters the prized horns of the Etraxavax occasionally rising above the surface. Because of the unique properties of their horns and teeth they were used in many Kravjin ceremonies and Eronash rituals. *I wonder how Etraxavax taste.* His stomach growled at the thought. *Eating will have to wait. I have more important matters to attend to.* He was close enough now to hear the dripping of water from the fangs and talons of the dragon effigies. Everyone knew to be cautious and not let the water drip on them because it became toxic after making contact with the dragon images. This was by design of course, and the water was collected in vessels that could hold it safely. He shuddered as he recalled the ways the waters were used—on those who deserved it, of course.

Finally, he stood at the unique gates made of materials from the realms of Creminmorta. His extrasensory powers told him that he was being observed and he casually gazed up. The green and black scales lining the gates began to shift and increase in size. In a flash of a moment, a single yellowish eye appeared in the center of the scales, then it vanished into the now black viscous substance of the gate. The gates swung open inward, and he looked closely into the thick, black, multi-dimensional material of the gates as he passed and saw grey mist-like faces of various humanoids. *Kaogreem?* The origins of the mist-like beings were a mystery. Legend had it that they were once corporeal beings.

His musings broke off as he heard the Houssadoom gates close behind him. He looked admiringly at a row of Adremesys trees with their beautiful charcoal outer bark. Splashes of luminous reds and blues showed him glimpses of the Tharamander lizards skittering about in the trees. The colors of the lizards were a warning of the toxic enzymes secreted after consuming the leaves. The enzymes were used in certain Eronash rituals as well. The trees themselves only produced fruit once every fifteen years, so he was amazed to see budding fruit on the branches. *I wonder what that would taste like.* Immediately, he was disturbed that his mind was losing the battle against the base needs of his flesh. *I suppose I am hungrier than I want to believe.*

"I better keep moving," he said, noticing the silhouette of a Gremingard capital ship about two kilometers to the west. It hovered over the Kravjin military base. Below the ship, the sun's rays reflected off the body armor of hundreds of Krauvanok sorcerer legionnaires, who stood in parade formation. *New Grauvagogs, elite commandos, protectors of the Gremingards.* He was very impressed by the distinct Creminstüka energy, which powered the Gremingard and its forces. The entrance to the temple was protected by a semi-transparent shield.

A high-ranking temple guard emerged from behind the shield. "Greetings, Lord Khanon." He executed a sharp military salute. "Follow me to the council chamber." The guard spun in place then vanished behind the shield again. Khanon took sure steps through the masking field, quickly following.

Khanon felt all eyes on him as he made his way into the room where Chi Ku Ren, the Kravjin supreme leader, sat in the center of a semi-circle formation. He noted that Adad Mahath was among the thirty-eight Qwravasha priests as he made his way to his seat.

The smell of sulfur hit his nose, and his eyes began to water. *He is here.* He stiffened, hoping the slither of fear did not show on his face as he sat down hard. *I am a dead man.*

A moment later, illuminated symbols and images from the book of Eronash created a small circle in the center of the floor, then quickly expanded outward. The center became a pool of silver liquid. Emerging from it were several wisps of black smoke with red and yellowish eyes that were immediately followed by two large black wings. The Spectrarex's hooved feet hovered atop the shimmering pool. Its powerful wings extended outward and then retracted back, folding against its back. The smaller wisps of black mist were the Nossorads that now swirled around the chamber. In unison they all stood and then knelt on the ground with their foreheads touching the floor in reverence and fear.

Chi Ku Ren raised himself up off the ground. "How can we serve you, Master Abaddon?"

"By grand design the Leviathans were to be sealed in a multiphasic vortex, each within the five galaxies to be released in the age to come, as it is written in the book of Eronash. For now, until further notice, it is forbidden to venture into those vortexes where the five Leviathan races are now held." Abaddon's gnarled, clawed hands rose in the air. "Rise to your feet!" The booming command caused everyone to hurriedly do as he said.

The familiar Nossorads swirled around the Spectrarex's head. His menacing glare scanned the priests and then stopped to Khanon's far left.

"Nothing escapes the all-seeing eye… Nebesh Gwauth!" the beast shouted. Energy erupted out of his hand and arced onto the surface of the chamber. A dark, oblong shape emerged from the floor. On either side of the hovering object were two Qwravasha priests who landed on their feet after being released by the Nossorads. Khanon eyes widened a little; he had never seen this Creminmorta object in person.

The mighty Spectrarex extended his right, clawed finger toward them. "Your true loyalties lie with your superiors in the KMI." His clawed hands sparked with energy. "Temgwa Nebeth," He spoke a second Toxrokk command, and immediately a single Nossorad's sharp talons wrapped around one of the priest's upper body. The priest issued a blood-curdling scream of terror and anguish, and his clothes began to smolder. The semi-transparent Nossorad brought the helpless priest to the onyx object and then threw him against it. The object absorbed him. The mighty Spectrarex glared at the remaining priest, whose face was to the floor. "Rise, Agent Penna, tell your superiors that your peer is now in the abyss of Baracurra. If they do not heed their lord's command not to venture into or near the five Leviathan vortexes, they will surely join him. Now, leave us and do not return. Your life is spared...for now."

Without hesitation, Penna bowed reverently. "Thank you, Lord and Master Abaddon." The shaken priest quickly gathered his composure and left the inner chamber.

Back to the KMI Regional Inquisitors Office, no doubt, Khanon thought with derision. At that moment, Khanon felt a weight lift off his shoulders at the realization that the destruction of the Leviathan project was foreseen and was accounted for in the ages to come. He was relieved. *The Tisrad Dragon possesses such foresight and intelligence beyond comprehension.* "Truly a god," he murmured.

He didn't realize he'd spoken aloud until Abbadon's cold, lifeless stare fell upon him. "Khanon, your carnal mind cannot fathom strategies that span millennia, for you are mortal. We are eternal... yet I will honor you with another task to be revealed in the time I choose." The Spectrarex then addressed the chamber at large. "Kravanoblus will soon commence the creation of a new order, one that will challenge the Order of Marium Kahnet and ensure the emergence of the Krevomax; the Tisrad messiah. The purging of the new religion on Shalem has begun. Your new orders are to completely eradicate this upstart religion based on a false messiah and redeemer of creation. Wherever he is. For there is only one god, Kravanoblus!"

The massive beast's black wings retracted and folded around his body as he descended back into the silver pool. Just as it was completely submerged, a stream of dark shadows erupted outward, then disappeared through the chamber walls and the ceiling. The tension and fear in the room vanished with the beast.

Chi Ku Ren moved in front of Khanon and stared piercingly into his eyes. "I understand that your plan to eliminate this new religion on Shalem has already begun." He scowled darkly in displeasure.

"Yes, it has." Khanon preened slightly as he tugged his clothing back in place. "As planned, the government of Shalem will soon join the Varkrato league," Khanon said confidently.

"Your life was forfeit with the destruction of the Leviathan project." Ren's voice was harsh with a thread of anger. "But since Lord Abaddon has spared you and has his eye on you, we will decide on alternative punishment for allowing the enemy to infiltrate a level one security project." Khanon felt his heart begin to pound heavily. "For now you will go on your way. Be sure that your resources do not fail to eradicate this new religion on Shalem... You are dismissed, Lord Khanon."

The dire threat was clear, and Khanon could feel the power emanating from Ren in the silent chamber. He bowed in respect to the supreme leader, and left the chamber straightaway to meet with Mindendra.

Khanon peered through the transparent metal window atop the upper section of the KMI Regional Inquisitors headquarters in the center of Kurjafa. He thought about his wife's expression of concern when he'd informed her that he had to attend another official meeting before coming home. *I am blessed to have such a supportive, caring wife.* His heart swelled with love for her.

Sensing the approach of someone, he turned to the door of the spacious room, which was just then sliding open. He smiled widely. "Congratulations, Mindendra, on your promotion to Praetor Inquisitor, and your re-assignment here on my home world." He gazed admiringly at the new uniform worn only by High Command KMI Officers.

"Thank you Lord Khanon, it will be a pleasure working with you again." Her right hand touched the top of her left hand, and the sound of energized particles crackled and echoed in the room as a purplish semi-transparent force field enveloped them. "I was pleasantly surprised that your life was spared after the Leviathan project was destroyed." The relief in her voice sounded genuine. "We have been informed about the visit of Abbadon and his instructions regarding the Leviathan vortexes. Of course, that mandate will be carried out without any exceptions. On another matter, what happened to Captain Draxrad? The ship never exploded like the others. Is he alive somewhere? And what about the Hedropex spheres?" Her words seemed to run together, she spoke so quickly.

"Those are legitimate questions. Some of which I believe I can find answers to. All we need is to find a common thread." He nodded reassuringly with a slight semblance of a smile. "Now, then, I am sure you have been informed that there is a new Order of women that will challenge the Marium Kahnet. Apparently this new Order will usher in the arrival of the Krevomax." His voice held a note of excitement. He crossed his arms, tapping one index finger on his bicep. "Maybe that is why my ship and Captain Draxrad's ship were not destroyed. The promised Tisrad messiah, no less, would need a lot of power."

"Yes, I believe your assumption is correct. This new Order is the key to unlocking the clues to your ship's whereabouts." Mindendra's tone indicated the depth of her belief, which matched his own.

"I believe you are right. I must make the acquaintance of the founders of this new sect. Maybe they can lead me to Captain Draxrad, but more importantly to the Hedropex spheres aboard my ship." His eyes gleamed with fresh vigor at the thought. "I have a promising place to look for the person who is capable of forming this new religious Order." A big smile split his somewhat gaunt cheeks.

"Who?"

"Princess Rishna Atharva, who has been receiving a group of highly skilled female sorceresses on her home planet, Gerobon, in the Kilodromus galaxy," he said, smug that he knew this little known fact.

"And why do you think that these particular sorceresses are the architects behind this new female Order?" Her skepticism was one of the things he liked about her.

"These women are not ordinary sorceresses. They are exclusively from the royal families among our allies, throughout the five galaxies of the Quintástraya. Princess Atharva serves as the high priestess of the Order of Aggrevox."

"Very interesting, Lord Khanon," she drawled, tapping her finger against her chin. "You just might have something there. Now on another matter, it is being reported, but has not been confirmed, that your associates have terminated the family of the false messiah on Shalem." Mindendra peered narrowly into his eyes.

Khanon smiled wide. "Yes, it's true, I sent some of my best assets in an effort to sway the Shalem government to join the Varkrato League."

"My orders from KMI supreme headquarters are to observe and assist with the Shalem government transition as an ally. Thankfully, it will not be very difficult, seeing that the large death tolls on Letalis and Necropis have swayed the public's opinion away from the Mantis Alliance." Her smile was victorious.

"Indeed, it seems what appeared to be disastrous to me at first has turned out to be very beneficial for all of us. The sacrifice of tens of millions on Letalis and Necropis has caused dozens of neutral governments to join us for protection." His definitive statement was met with her nod of agreement.

"The gods have given you great favor, Lord Khanon!" Her eyes were full of admiration. Mindendra's ear twitched, indicating she had heard his grumbling stomach. "It seems you are famished to see your wife and family," she said jokingly.

"Yes, you are right, I am. Now then, I will send you a report about the gathering in Gerobon." His eyes smiled approvingly at her.

"I will reciprocate with a detailed report regarding the upstart religion on Shalem. I need that sect to be completely crushed into the pages of history," she said with an air of determination. At his accepting nod, she touched her left hand, once more disengaging the privacy force field.

"Have a safe journey, Praetor Inquisitor." Khanon gave her a slight bow.

"Enjoy your time with your wife and family, Lord Khanon." She responded in kind, then headed out of the room.

Khanon's mind raced with the sad task of informing his brother that his daughter had been in the Leviathan project when it was destroyed. Yet for some reason he had a strong sense that she was not dead. He had always felt such a connection with her. She was more like him then her own father.

"Maybe she survived like Captain Draxrad," he murmured. "Maybe I will just tell him that she is trapped within the Leviathan vortex, which is off limits to all, no exceptions…" He nodded, making up his mind. "That will have to do for now. It's time to go home."

Chapter Seven

REDIQUIN

Waves of the Cremindraux radiation that swept across the surface of Necropis had incapacitated Rediquin's ship's cloaking and shielding systems. With the shields offline, the *Furies Scepter* had been exposed and detected by an orbital security station. She was now desperately evading capture by a trio of security drones.

Screaming through narrow crevasses deep within the Necropis mantle, the *Furies Scepter* darted, spun, and sped deeper into uncharted caverns. One of the drones struck the tip of a sharp rock and was instantly destroyed, but the other two doggedly kept pace with her. Out of the corner of her eye she saw a flashing warning from a small display to her left.

"Too late," she exclaimed through gritted teeth.

The large eruption of magma that the sensor had warned her about hit the edge of the wing of her ship, knocking it off course toward a field of jutting super-heated rocks. She fought to keep control of the ship and was vaguely aware of the incineration of the two drones by the same explosion of lava. "Aahhhhhh… No!"

she yelled as she used all of her flying skills to avoid smashing into the rock spires.

Her body jerked as the ship grazed the towering rocks, scraping loudly between two of the spires. Most of the control displays where offline, but she breathed a deep sigh of relief as she steered the ship away from the roiling sea of lava. "Thank you, Abba El," she said, wiping the sweat from her brow with the back of her gloved hand. Her body hummed with adrenaline and alarm. "I need to find a way out of here." She was anxious and frustrated, but she took a deep breath and forced herself to relax. *I entered a dead volcano range surrounded by a sea of ice. I must be somewhere in the cold southern regions of Tamsaram.* She burst out in ironic laughter, because the region was bitterly cold. "That surely is the story of my life… raging heat or icy cold."

A thread of hope began to surface in her spirit as she travelled through a large tunnel where rivers of lava had once flowed. "It's getting cooler. Good, it looks as though I will find a way out of here." She clasped her hands together in thankfulness. She noticed a flat surface just ahead and immediately landed to take stock of the damage.

"Let's check the goods." She hurriedly examined the state of her Cymbratar. "Still sparkling like the precious gems they are." Smiling, she exhaled a deep sigh of relief that they hadn't been affected by the Cremindraux radiation inside the protective containment box. The sequence of miniscule events of good fortune lifted her spirits.

Standing up, she pressed her nose against the side viewport to see geysers of steam making contact with the hot rock surfaces. "I hope that is seawater." Her voice echoed in the stillness of the cabin. She could hear the settling of the ship, clicking and groaning.

She rebooted the internal and external sensors and sifted through a plethora of data that lit up the screens. Just as she had suspected, the outer hull had sustained substantial damage. She was grateful that she had added class two Kelkatanium armor plating to the ship when she had purchased it. "Yes, that is seawater, and my way out." Her fisted hand shot in the air victoriously. Immediately she prepared to leave the cavern through the gushing geysers. *What a rush. I think I'm addicted to life as a mercenary.*

Before leaving, she made herself eat a TEPP ration. "Well then, here we go…"

The ship lifted off and boldly plunged into the violent streams of rushing seawater. She gripped the manual flight controls tightly as she broke through the opening of a fissure in the deep-sea trench, releasing tension as she flew across the roiling waves. Her initial scans indicated that she was near one of the oldest and coldest cities in the southern hemisphere, Tomongusta.

She pursed her lips. "I hope I can find cloaking components." A prick of guilt about her quest of revenge upon her enemies struck her as she correlated in her mind her own intentions with the tens of millions of causalities caused by the destruction of the Stadageo that others had actually committed. *How many deaths will it take to satisfy my revenge?* She quickly squelched any sense of remorse. "Until all our enemies are dead… that is how many." Her face hardened, turning as rigid and cold as ice. Back to business, she monitored the local ship traffic communications frequencies and concluded that the increased traffic was due to the mass evacuations caused by the moving toxic clouds of radiation.

The night sky was dotted with lights heading toward Tomongusta, and she decided to join a small cluster of low flying ships. "I hope their sensors were damaged like mine." Her nose scrunched up as she smelled the stale air in the cabin and altered her flight path just as the ships passed her position. Rediquin continued monitoring their communications. "I don't understand why there is so much damage with the destruction of the Stadageo." She frowned, trying to reason it out.

"If Zeta Three's employers can obtain the same power for their Stadageo, they could cause vastly more destruction." She shook her head, regretting she had exchanged Cymbratar for detailed plans to build a Stadageo back at the market. She pressed her lips together and determinedly set the thoughts aside. Instead, she rehearsed her every move and possible contingencies to make her escape if necessary. She landed with several other ships in a large transportation bay, and quickly powered down.

"I better get my gear," she grumbled and made her way to the cargo, where she slipped on her subzero rated gloves and overcoat. Placing an extra power cell for her AR-57 energy pistol, she stood silent for a moment, letting her well-trained mind and body focus on what was ahead. *I am as ready as I will ever be.* She exited, touching a small metal band around her wrist that sent an encrypted message to the local Choshek agent network, of her location and need of assistance.

The cold air blew strongly against her face, and she shivered. A large cloud of white mist from her breath as it hit the near freezing temperature in the terminal wafted over her head as she walked, and she quickly activated the face shield. Her body temperature was slow to adjust even though she wore a bio-thermic body skin suit. She joined a group of passengers leaving a nearby transport, blending in with the similar-looking humanoid beings. They were talking animatedly amongst themselves and did not pay any attention to her.

Rediquin quietly boarded a shuttle heading to the oldest section of Tomongusta, where she hoped she could avoid the authorities and find parts for her ship. Her light enhancement optic visor gave her a clear view of the sea cliffs set against the bright moon in the cloudless dark sky. The shuttle made its way through the thick forest of luminescent, deep blue, crystalline spires. The spires were a natural barrier between the original settlement of the mostly abandoned ice city of Glacia and Tomongusta Prime. She could barely make out the remains of the original walls constructed by the Terrodrak, the architects and engineers of all the ice continent's settlements. The forefathers could not have known when they first came to build in the rich mineral ice regions that they would become one of the most frequented areas of the deadly giant, Mogwatto.

It was the Mogwatto breeding season in the dead of winter here. The settlers' first attempts to defend themselves against the massive sea creatures' thick exoskeleton—made of naturally produced Essallanium that was as hard as class three Mantatonium plating— was largely unsuccessful. The ability to expel bursts of high-energy plasma coupled with their sheer size of over two hundred meters in height made them nearly impossible to kill. They were bar none one of the largest and dangerous predators in this region of the galaxy.

Near a sparsely populated section of the nearly abandoned old settlement, her visor lit up with a blinking red dot indicating an incoming encrypted code and message. Her spirit leapt when the red dot turned green. *Good, I have made contact with a Choshek operative.*

The shuttle stopped at the terminal. She tapped her overcoat, where her weapon was hidden, and strode down the ramp, directly onto the hard ice-covered ground. She cautiously followed behind several others in between the antiquated and partially dilapidated superstructures, seemingly held together by a patchwork of hurried repairs by the locals. Screeching from above made her aware of half a dozen Mossavento sea scavengers that were swooping threateningly low. She palmed her weapon and tugged the sleeve of her coat over it to hide the barrel, and lengthened her strides to reach a merchant trading post just ahead.

Rediquin determined the seemingly solid entrance to the trading post was a standard nano wall, and walked right through it. The interior temperature was a bit more tolerable and she began to look at the offerings of locally caught food near the entrance. She held her breath at the waft of rotted food and other foul odors that assaulted her senses through her face protection. It was a far cry from the hot humid air and pleasant odors of the Aphasium marketplace.

Scanning the layout of her surroundings, she headed toward the center, where small islands of mining and fishing equipment were displayed. "Here we go, let's see what I can find back there." A puff of white misted the interior of her visor as she spoke aloud. Several rows of new and used parts for machines that miners used in this region were stacked near the back wall. A crawling sensation made her aware that she had caught someone's attention. She peered out of the side of her eyes without turning her head, to see one of three stocky men purchasing mining equipment on her left staring at her. He nodded at her, then turned away. *They are brave, but they're out of their mind.* It was a dangerous vocation to venture onto the sea cliffs and retrieve the rare Bordroxium mineral. Especially at this time, when the Mogwatto fed on the unique minerals during their breeding cycle. *I better get moving.*

Using longer strides than usual, she reached the rows of engine parts. Most of the used parts seemed to need repairs, so she passed over them. She was perusing some old common engine core components, most of which also looked in need of repair, when a shadow approached from her right. Her hand darted to her energy pistol and she turned to face the thinly clothed Shevadranian, who by their very nature preferred cold climates. The small, unmasked, blue and neon green-skinned female gazed right at her, then nodded slightly, moving past.

Relaxing marginally, Rediquin turned her attention back to an interesting universal auxiliary power-coupling regulator that she just might be able to use. Just then, her visor lit up with an encrypted message and the cipher keys in her visor quickly unlocked it:

You are in danger. Head to the very back wall and go to the door marked with a small blue star on the top right corner, immediately. End of transmission.

"Would you like to purchase that?" the monotone voice of an old automaton attendant spoke from the end of the aisle.

"Price?" Rediquin's' voice was muffled by her protective visor.

"Twenty-five hundred units."

Without replying, she continued to examine the part, waiting for the attendant to leave. A loud noise from near the entrance caught the automaton's attention and it glided away.

She laid down the ship component, then crept to the edge of the mining machines and saw three individuals dressed in full military combat gear at the entrance. Sensing that trouble may be headed her way, she slowly started walking backwards, keeping her eyes fixed on them. Her senses were accurate; a firefight broke out between the guards and several others who were fighting their way out of the establishment. *Those people must be mercenaries or agents, maybe both.* "Find the door in the back," she whispered, and took the cover of the fray in the other part of the building to dash to the back of the store.

With weapon in hand, she swiftly made her way to a curtain in the back corner and passed through it. She could hear the firefight intensifying. "No blue star," she said as she sprinted along a curved wall with several doors.

"There it is," she said victoriously.

She removed her glove and placed her hand on the center of the door's cold surface. It slid open. She quickly replaced her glove as she walked through it. The noise of the firefight ceased as the door slid shut behind her. She realized that she had entered a transportation platform, which immediately began to descend. It seemed somewhat unstable, as it made an unsettling amount of noise.

"Now the question is, who has contacted me? I hope they have extra components to fix my cloaking systems." She shook her head, feeling pessimistic. Her body swayed with the jerking motion of the platform coming to a halt. It was enough to knock her off her feet. From a kneeling position, she swung the weapon from right to left, searching for a target.

"Don't shoot, Rediquin, it's me." A familiar voice spoke from the shadows and echoed in the cave. Zeta Three stepped into the dim light.

Relieved, she rose to her feet, slid the hood off her head, and retracted her visor. "I thought you went off world to make a delivery." She slid the weapon back into its holster at her side, and stepped off the platform. The tone of her white skin was emphasized by the darkness of her clothing. Her high cheekbones were rosy with the warmth of adrenaline that was just beginning to fade.

"No one is going to come down here." He quickly made his way to the platform behind her and deactivated it. Although he was a highly trained mercenary, he was not impervious to the charms of the opposite sex. He gazed deeply into her large, light blue eyes. It was clear to her that a part of his soul was being drawn to her. "I never noticed how beautiful your eyes are," he said almost in a whisper. He seemed to come to his senses, and stepped away from her. "Look, I helped you escape capture, now I need your help getting Bordroxium ore." His blunt statement was more of a demand than a request.

"Thanks, that's a great move shutting off that platform. It's a menace," she joked to lighten the mood. "Now the only thing that will kill me is a Mogwatto. We are at the sea cliffs, aren't we?" She deliberately ignored his demand for the moment, trying to discern him.

Without a reply, he turned and strode toward a hollowed-out section of deep blue ice some dozen meters away. Noting she was not following, he stopped and motioned for her to move. "Hurry, we don't have much time."

She vaguely appreciated the rich baritone of his voice as it echoed into the other mining shafts. Shaking off the layers of meaning in the short encounter, she made her way to his side. His gloved hands glided over a holographic panel.

"I will give you the names that I know of the rogue sisters that are on Letalis, Necropis, and Tartarus. But first I need your word that you will help me get some Bordroxium ore," he said. "I am going to need the mineral where I am going. Rediquin, I don't trust anyone else on Necropis. Besides, I know that you have vested interested in finding them, namely a large reward."

She pressed her lips together, but said nothing. He swallowed as if coming to a decision, and he shut the door behind them. A strange look came over his face. She suddenly became aware they were standing in a mining scavenger ship. Before she could protest, he was in the pilot's seat and her body was swaying as they exited the tunnel. Her fears were confirmed about his strange look as they burst into the dawn's early light. She slid her weapon carefully out of its holster and remained standing, waiting.

"I don't recall agreeing to help you," she angrily challenged with nostrils flaring. Her potentially deadly intent was evident in her strong stance.

"If you shoot me, it will take you a very long time to find out who the rogues are in order to save their lives." He remained silent as they veered toward a large curved section of the cliffs, where the Mogwatto seemed to be active. She noted that the old settlement would soon be in the bellies of the Mogwatto as she wrestled with being taken somewhere against her will.

"I am sure you have seen the destructiveness of the Cremindraux radiation," she said finally, glaring into his eyes. "Is the Bordroxium mineral to be used to power a Stadageo?" She conceded just then, with a dramatic holstering of her weapon to let him know of her reluctance.

"Yes, it's not nearly as powerful as those energy spheres Overseer Khanon used, but it will do. But now I am on a most urgent matter that necessitates that I leave immediately for the Malgavatta galaxy… more specifically, the Fortuu Expanses."

That is where I was heading, she thought, looking at him with narrowed eyes.

"I know that one of the sisters has been captured by my associates on the Letalis moon." He glanced at her set expression. "It is Victoria Maja, a Synogog member no less. Nia and Taona will soon join her." She was surprised that he knew so much.

"I need the rest of those names, so let's get done quickly. I don't want to end up in the belly of a Mogwatto," she said as he landed the small craft in a generous outcropping in the cliff's face. He activated his protective headgear and she immediately followed suit. Wasting no time, he gave her quick instructions on how to find and extract the mineral using the bulky piece of equipment he placed into her arms.

"We will not have a lot of time to mine before a Mogwatto senses the ore we have extracted. As soon as the mineral finding indicator reaches three bars, stop and let me know," he said. "Three bars, no less." He waited until she nodded yes.

As instructed, she followed the red dot on the small display panel to where a streak of the ore seemed to be. Standing still for a moment, she surveyed the area. "Great, if a Mogwatto shows up, there is no way of escape," she said dryly as she set to work.

"I can hear you." His lightly mocking tone rang loudly in her ear. She gave a wry grimace, and was glad he couldn't see it. "Now, then, I must tell you that there is a senior Choshek agent named Medon Sotasen who has been given charge of the search for the sisters on Letalis on behalf of Overseer Khanon."

This information went a long way to appease her anger at his manipulating her into helping him. She began to work more quickly, getting the hang of using the device.

"I've never heard of a senior agent of another clan have the authority to hunt traitors on another clan's home turf," she said, raising an eyebrow. Her Cymbratar-induced, computer-like memory failed to put a face to the name. "Hhmmm." She hoped to be able to find other rogues who had not been captured.

"I suspect that Agent Sotasen will have reported to Dargo Sanwolf, the senior Overseer on Letalis." He paused for a moment, then said knowingly, "That should give you plenty of time to find them."

"I accept your peace offering..." She knew she would wonder

what he was up to later. "What do you know of Liberation Shalem?" She probed, changing the subject.

"From what I have gathered, the Varkrato league is trying to add members through subversion. As you well know, this sector of space is very unstable. Nothing should surprise you." She could hear a scraping noise from the tool that he was using. "Great, I have two bars," he exclaimed.

"I have one and a half bar," she replied. A menacing shiver slid up and down her spine. It made her very aware of the danger they were in. She looked around, waiting for the monstrous sea creatures to appear.

"Who are the sisters here on Necropis?" His steady voice in her ear was just what she needed. She took a moment to maneuver her equipment deeper into a splintered section of rock.

"Their names are Orisa and Mirinda." She could feel the ache of her shoulders from holding the bulky machine steady. Her voice held a note of strain as she divulged the secret to him. "They are currently operating as Choshek agents here on Necropis. Why do you care?" She let a thread of sarcasm bleed through to test him.

"I have my reasons. But between you and me, let's say I am not fond of the Synogog or the Kravjin. To be perfectly honest, I am pleased that the Stadageos were destroyed." With this open dialog between them, she felt trust begin to grow stronger.

"Well then, it looks as though you will have to find Fay first, since Nia and Taona are on an assignment for Dukar Gruppa," he said with a sly smirk in his voice.

"Fay… Are there any others?" She huffed as she moved the mining equipment along the mineral vein.

"No there are not, and Fay is in one of the safe houses in Ausertane. You know the place." He grunted with effort as he wedged the mining tool into a narrow crevasse.

"Yes, I know the one. I am impressed with your intelligence gathering abilities." She was grateful for the wealth of information he had willingly imparted, and felt a sense of companionship she had not felt in a great while.

"Being in our particular trade, one needs as many resources in just as many places as possible. To save you time, I will give you her exact location after we leave here." He stopped speaking and she could hear the grinding of the machine.

"I appreciate that," she yelled over the noise of both machines. The sense of danger again impinged on her spirit. She quivered at the thought of encountering a Mogwatto. The bulky machine bucked in her hands and vibrated strongly as it bored up to her elbows into the rock-hard surface of the frozen trace mineral bearing wall. .

"I have two bars!" she said excitedly. Pulling back, letting the tool rest for a moment, she looked out into the open sea. In the distance were more mining scavengers clinging to the face of the cliffs. *Fools, oh, look who's talking,* she mocked herself.

"Rediquin, I am increasing the power to my machine so that I can extract the ore faster. But be aware it may draw the attention of the beasts." His voice held a thread of urgency now.

"Okay, I will do the same." She had a strong feeling their time to get the ore and get out safely was drawing very near. She stretched her back, trying to get the stiffness out, then continued extracting information from him. "Are there any rogue sisters on Tartarus?"

"The only rogue there is someone named Balese. She hasn't been found yet, but it is a certainty that she will eventually be caught and publicly executed. Hey, I have reached three bars, how about you?"

"Yes, I am at three." She could hear him shut off his equipment, and she followed suit. *If not death by a sea monster, surely by some other horrible way. Maybe that should be my fate. I guess I will see my family and old friends soon enough.* Rediquin thought she was losing her balance on the ice but was alarmed to see a row of large horns in the distance breaking the surface of the sea. "Mogwatto!" she yelled, yanking back on the drilling machine and almost dropping it.

"Don't leave your machine, bring it with you. Hurry, Rediquin, I don't want to lose you." His alarmed voice gave her new strength. She gripped the machine with both hands, held it to her body, and sprinted to the ship.

"Zeta Three, I am in. Let's go!" The door shut behind her. He had activated the engines, but they were not moving. "Why are we still here? The Mogwatto out there is only a few kilometers away!" she said with urgency.

"I believe there might be one even closer." His voice was sharp with excitement at the danger. She watched his hands fly over the controls. It was only after they lifted off that she released the breath she had been holding and made herself calm down.

Just then, they spotted a fully-grown Mogwatto, tearing at the cliffs just below them. The powerful energy bursts that shot from it broke up the rock-hard cliffs. It turned its massive head toward them. "It can smell the Bordroxium minerals in the mining equipment," she said, awed at its magnificence, but her admiration was quelled at its attention on them. Zeta Three was maneuvering the scavenger ship away as fast as he could, but the glow on the horns of the beast indicated it was ready to discharge a burst of plasma at them. "Can this ship go any slower?" Her frustrated question drew a sharp bark of laughter from him.

"Don't worry, half of the ships that get attacked survive." The comment did nothing to ease her concern.

He glided toward safety as fast as he could. Just as they cleared the range of the Mogwatto attacking from below, another reared its massive body from the top of cliff. It shot a blast of energy with deadly accuracy. Reacting swiftly, he managed to avoid the brunt of it, but the immense force of the blast repelled the ship with incredible speed toward the tip of a jutting rock on the icy mountainside.

"We have lost primary flight control!" he shouted as he fought to adjust the thrusters to gain some control of the trajectory. It appeared for a moment that he had some success. He grimly shouted, "Hold on, we are going to crash in minus five, four, three, two—" His voice was cut off.

Her head slammed forward and then back as the scavenger ship crashed violently into the snow-covered mountainside.

Overcome with urgency, she removed the laughable excuse for safety straps on the co-pilot seat, and exited the still intact ship.

With her energy pistol at the ready, she prepared to encounter the ugly beast. Kilometers away, a few Mogwattos were basking in the sunlight. She turned to see Zeta Three emerge from the ship, and they stood without speaking a word, gazing at the sea monsters. The pitiful scavenger ship was partially submerged in a pool of icy water. "Once the water freezes, it will be much harder to break it free." She knew they would have very little success in getting the ship out if they waited.

"Don't worry. I told you I am prepared for such emergencies. Rescue is on its way." His tone was smug. He extended his arm and placed his fingertips on his wristband. Like a mirage, a small ship de-cloaked twenty meters away. "My ship also has cloaking capabilities." He bowed dramatically and motioned for her to follow him. She rolled her eyes and stiffly moved forward.

He settled into his pilot's seat and returned her gaze. "What?" he asked dismissively.

"I assume you have the Bordroxium bars?" She shook her head in disbelief. *Wow, he is good.* She felt a genuine admiration for him begin to grow.

"Yep." He removed his gloves and entered new flight coordinates.

Sitting in the plush co-pilot's seat, she retracted her visor back into the headgear to get a better look at his ship. "A Mark 5 Series. You must have gotten a good deal on it," she said with appreciation as she strapped herself in.

"I am assuming you will need to get back to your repaired ship, right?" he said, smirking and ignoring her comment.

"Repaired, what are you talking about?" Her tone was ripe with suspicion and a veiled threat.

"Relax Rediquin, I intercepted your network beacon. You did sent out your assist code, remember?" He smiled, looking at her with raised brows. "It was marked as contaminated with radiation and was taken along with several other ships to a quarantine bay, scheduled to be decontaminated. So, I contacted some of my associates who happen to work within those ship bays. While we were mining, your ship was repaired. That, by the way, includes the cloaking systems."

His confidence was annoying, but the help was welcome. "But the cloaking systems of the *Furies Scepter* are more advanced than the components used on yours," she protested, hating the thought of having inferior parts used on her cherished prize.

"I use newer cloaking components. So I had some sent over to be installed on yours. Very expensive, as you know." His smile vanished as he concentrated on flying. He went quiet as he maneuvered the ship through the narrow spaces between tall and thin ice plateaus.

"Thank you," she said quietly.

"You owe me big." He turned his head and caught the fresh burgeoning anger in her eyes. She seethed with the thought of being indebted to anyone. It didn't help that she was beginning to be attracted to him.

"How about as payment I give you a shipment of Cymbratar, and we will call it even?" Her tone was carefully controlled.

"Let me think about that for a moment while I make my approach." A series of manufacturing complexes, just outside

Tomongusta Prime appeared below them.

She cupped her hand over her mouth to capture some of the heat, waiting for the cabin to warm. "It's a rather large stash. Enough to purchase replacement parts for your cloaking system upgrades several times over." She would have no choice but to reveal one of the locations where she hid her emergency reserves on Necropis if he accepted.

After landing his ship on the ice-covered landing platform next to the *Furies Scepter*, which was covered by a canopy, he turned and looked piercingly into her eyes. "Not that I don't trust you, but are you willing to offer me a red marker?" It was the only way he could be certain she was telling the truth. No one offered a red marker and then rescinded a verbal agreement. If a red marker was given, and broken due to a lie from the person offering it, that person could be killed by anyone without any retribution.

"Yes… I always keep my word. If I tell you where the treasure is located, we are even…agreed?" Her eyes widened with an unnamed plea for the answer she wanted.

He nodded. "Agreed." He extended his open hand toward her.

Rediquin retrieved a small red disc from her pocket and touched it to her lips. "Deal," she said and placed it in the palm of his hand. She watched his long fingers close over the marker. His eyebrows lifted with a look of satisfaction. *That doesn't feel too bad.* An image of a rosy-cheeked, silky dark-haired child that might be theirs appeared in her mind's eye. Her head jerked back in surprise of her long dead desire's re-emergence. *I can't think about that now.*

"Deal," he said and watched her as she stood up out of the seat.

"I will wait here until I receive the location." His face wore a look of appreciation and something else that was unmistakable. A twinge of attraction flared in her heart that she quickly shoved to the side.

She leaned over the lit console between them and placed a small green metallic ball on the control panel. "The coordinates and information will be sent to this communications sphere. You will have it shortly." She looked at him, not sure how she felt about the whole thing. "Until next time Zeta Three, thanks." She offered him a smile with genuine warmth, then activated her visor and adjusted her subzero gear as she made her way to the back of the ship. The door slid open and she jumped out, sinking ankle deep into the snow-covered ground.

Once inside her ship just a short distance away, she conducted a quick systems and power core diagnostic. "Everything seems to be in working order," she said, relieved.

She engaged the cloaking device to test it. A rare feeling of warmth and acceptance slid into her heart as she sent the encrypted message containing the location and information needed to retrieve the much-prized Cymbratar to Zeta Three. She smiled widely as she received the coordinates to Fay's location.

"He is very good looking for a human man." She laughed lightly. "Unfortunately, I don't have time for finding true love. Maybe in another lifetime." Her words didn't carry the same certainty that they used to.

She smiled wryly as she looked at the surface of the ice city of

Tomongusta, fading into the distance. "Fay is in the Ausertane continent, a rather warm place. I guess I should wear something more appropriate."

Chapter Eight

NECROPIS

After being rescued by Choshek operatives, Mirinda and Orisa were taken deep into the nefarious organization's lair. The utilitarian-style building they were brought to looked like a military bunker. But now it was a safe house for them, as they had just learned that the Necropis military—under the direction of the KMI—were executing entire families of those labeled as collaborators with the Stadageo saboteurs. The grim truth that their adopted families were killed just before they were rescued had hit them hard.

"How could this happen? Our families slaughtered along with thousands of others just because we work at the Stadageo...?" Orisa sobbed harshly, the reality of the far-reaching consequences of her actions was clearly setting in.

"This is a travesty. A perversion of justice with the stink of the Tisrad Dragon all over it." Mirinda's eyes were moist, but she held on to her composure. *I am glad my husband is dead. He was a rotten, self-centered man, and his sons and daughters were no different. They never accepted me. Serves him right, the unfaithful rodent.* Mirinda was surprised by her hard, steely heart. She moved over to the bench were Orisa sat hunched over in misery. "Orisa, get ahold of yourself. Here, let me fix that for you." Mirinda adjusted Orisa's makeshift ankle brace that looked like it was ready to fall off. "This will have to do until we can get you proper help." She stood and started pacing anxiously. "I should have risked taking some Cymbratar with us. You would have been healed by now." Her voice was filled with self-condemnation that was clearly more than just about the injury.

"Now what do we do?" Orisa said glumly. "Our plans did not account for this outcome. We were going to damage the Stadageo, then leave Necropis and never return. Now, we will never be able to start that new life on Ramah."

"Staying on Necropis is not an option. We need to leave as quickly as possible." Mirinda crossed her arms stubbornly. "They rescued us for a reason. Sure, our families were associates of the Choshek, but they did not rescue them, only us. And with all the chaos, why use resources to rescue us? Whatever the reason, we need to use it to secure a ship capable of traveling great distances."

Mirinda's mind was laser-focused on her objective: Return to Ramah and rebuild her legacy from the ashes of destruction.

The door to their room suddenly opened. A tall male agent with sharp narrow features entered. Two other guards remained outside.

"I come in the name of the Grand Dukar, Droden Namtar. As of now you will no longer be under Dukar Suun's rule." His high, nasal voice spoke of a cold cruelty that matched his face. "His greatness spared your lives in order to make you a proposal. One that you would be wise to accept." He sneered and placed his red orange stubby fingered hand on his holstered pistol in threat.

"We are grateful for the rescue. So yes, we would like to hear it." Mirinda looked at him with interest and hoped that he could not discern her distaste of him. Loud, muffled sounds broached the previously quiet building. *Sounds like civil unrest could lead to outbreaks of rebellion. We are not fighting a war for him, if that is what he wants from us.* Mirinda glanced toward Orisa, who stood and went to the single stark window in the room.

"Dukar Namtar offers you, in exchange for your specific skills and knowledge in taking part in a mission, a substantial favor in return. Anything you desire, within reason of course. All you have to do is enter a complex and help us identify and obtain components that will enhance our ability to fend off other networks vying for power." It was clear that he did not have a great deal of faith in these two rather unremarkable looking women. He cocked an eyebrow and tried to stare Mirinda down, testing her mettle.

"What is this complex and what components or systems do you want us to identify as useful to the Grand Dukar?" Orisa asked, drawing his provocative glare her way.

"We want Stadageo parts and components that are located in a high-security military facility. Those that could be used in one fashion or another to enhance shielding, weapons, sensors, and medical devices." His voice was void of emotion.

Mirinda and Orisa stared at each for a moment.

"Break into a high security facility to pilfer some parts to help the Grand Dukar. Sounds more like a suicide mission to me," Mirinda said with contrived derision, building her case for the big reward that would be due them. She turned a hard glare on him. "For payment we will want a Class III Galaxy Cruiser or something similar that can travel far distances without refueling."

His nostrils flared in response, but she remained boldly staring at him. "I accept your fee." He glanced at the brace on Orisa's ankle, then into her eyes. "You will stay here to properly attend to your injury." He returned his gaze to Mirinda with a small look of dawning respect. "One task for one ship." It was clear that he saw something in her that swayed his opinion of them.

"What assurance do I have that the Grand Dukar's word will be kept?" She narrowed her eyes at him.

"This is all you will need." He handed her a red marker that was a sacred bond in the Choshek organization. Now her eyebrows rose. This gesture meant they considered her and Orisa a part of the clan, not outsiders.

"Agreed. It is done." Mirinda slid the red marker into Orisa's utility belt. He offered his open hand and they clasped forearm to forearm, as was the custom.

The agent turned and looked at Orisa. "Follow those two guards just outside to the medical center. Mirinda, you will come with me to meet with the infiltration team. Don't worry about your friend, we are family after all." His tone was respectful.

"See you soon, Orisa." Mirinda placed her hand on her shoulder and squeezed gently.

Orisa smiled in kind. "Yes. Be careful." Her somber, hopeless tone would resonate in Mirinda's mind for a long while.

Mirinda popped the last of her TEPPS into her mouth. Her mind was far away, pondering the rumors of civil war spreading across Necropis. Her lips twisted as she concentrated on how she and Orisa could use the deep unrest that was sweeping across the land to their advantage, for their plan of escape.

"Approaching designated landing zone, prepare to disembark." The stern, commanding voice of Cindra, the mission leader, was loud and clear, snapping Mirinda out of her thoughts.

She adjusted her utility belt and concentrated on assessing the team's chance of success, which didn't seem likely. *Maybe I will make it out alive, maybe I won't.* She activated her face visor and welcomed the resurgence of energy that rushed through her body and mind from the food.

"Team, the Cremindraux radiation levels are at dangerously high, so we must penetrate the outer perimeter walls as quickly as possible." Cindra's tone exuded the confidence that only experience could impart. It was a common trait found in all senior Choshek operatives.

Mirinda's eyes darted to the top section of her visor. She read the screen showing the levels of radiation both inside and outside of the ship. *It will not take long for us to succumb to radiation poisoning, even with these sophisticated radiation-resistant body armor suits.* She felt a burgeoning dread of dying without knowing for certain that Fay and Orisa were safely on their way to Ramah.

"Red team. Prepare to disembark," Cindra barked from the cargo door, directing the team. "Hantak, make sure your team gets to the extraction zone on time." Cindra turned her attention to Mirinda, who was standing at the back of the cargo bay, watching the first group jump out of the ship. She motioned for her to approach. "Telfa Norr, stay by my side."

Mirinda nodded in acknowledgement. She had already become accustomed to her operative name, having rehearsed it over and over until it became second nature to respond to it.

"Let's hope you are as important as Dukar Suun says you are." It was obvious Cindra had not been informed how deeply she was involved at the Stadageo. Mirinda preferred to keep it that way.

She double-checked her military grade combat weapon. Her visor lit up with data indicating lethal levels of radiation, and her heart began to pound with dismay. In a flash of a moment the red team vanished.

"Ready, team? On my mark." Cindra was poised, with slightly bent knees, ready to leap out of the cargo bay onto the sea cliffs, just below. "Blue team. Now."

Mirinda grunted with the effort as she jumped out of the cargo bay. She landed with a thud on the outer perimeter pathway, half a step away from Cindra. The shadow of their ship vanished. The blue team quickly and stealthily moved toward the nearest entrance, protected by a level one force field.

"Telfa Norr, you're up." Cindra's low tone was muffled. She

moved to the side, allowing Mirinda access to an exposed power supply relay.

Mirinda immediately recognized the high-security control system and deftly set to work. In just a few short moments she had it disabled.

"Well done," Cindra said in a barely discernable undertone. It was clear she was impressed.

"Got it." Mirinda in a blur joined the rest of the team that had already entered the now open security gates. She mirrored Cindra's running strides and was relieved when the gates closed behind them. *The radiation is much less in here.* The narrow access way opened up to a chamber with connecting corridors. The team fanned out in defensive positions.

"Good. Red team has successfully disabled the internal and external sensors and monitoring systems." Cindra pulled several recon drone spheres from her belt, then continued in the same hushed voice, "Let's hope they also deactivated the guard droids as well." She launched the spheres down each of the corridors in short succession. Rising off her knees, Cindra pointed to the farthest corridor. "This way." Her voice trailed off as she set off. Mirinda easily kept pace beside her.

The entire team's visors were synced with the recon drones, two of which were now functioning as motion detectors within the corridors. One drone continued just ahead of them. Mirinda watched dozens of sentry droids patrolling the three prison complexes three hundred meters from their current position. *Apparently red team failed to deactivate the sentry droids. I should have been on that team instead. I would have made short work of it.* She knelt silently with the rest of the team, waiting.

Cindra soon spoke up: "It looks as though this is going to be a slightly more difficult task than we had anticipated. Nevertheless, we will go forward. Telfa Noor, you come with me. The rest of you know what to do. Remember mission protocols." Cindra didn't wait for anyone to reply, but rose to a crouch and activated the stealth mode of her body armor.

Mirinda followed suit, noting that Cindra blended subtly in with their surroundings. The power levels displayed on her visor indicated that the stealth function was only available for a short time. Her heartbeat quickened and her breathing shortened from the adrenaline rushing through her veins. She concentrated on following Cindra, who opened a panel in the floor and fell through it. With practiced determination she followed. *"Abba!"* she cried in her spirit as she plunged into the dark unknown.

She dipped into a fluid crouching position on the metal surface, absorbing the momentum of the controlled fall. Then she quickly stood, ready to fire if necessary. Noting Cindra was already running several dozen meters ahead of her, she broke into a fluid run. At the end of the corridor, Cindra signaled for caution with her hand. Just ahead, their visors indicated an auxiliary guard station, manned by two guards.

"I will take the one on my left, you take the one on your right, on three…" Cindra lifted her energized weapon.

Mirinda fought a very short battle with her conscience. *I thought all personnel had left because of the coming radiation clouds.* She lifted her own weapon, not pleased at having to shoot someone. *Now, I will really be a murderer.* The guards were oblivious to their presence, more focused on what they were looking at on their control screens.

"One...two ... three."

Cindra fired the first shot. A second later, Mirinda numbly watched her own target slump forward onto the station's control panel. The energized pellets had easily torn through the guard's thick uniforms. Cindra swiped a splash of blood off the display screen. "Can you disable the sentry droids from here?" she asked coldly.

"If I can access the main system cores, maybe." Mirinda was glad Cindra couldn't see the tears streaking down her cheeks. She held back a sniff, almost overcome with sadness at taking the life of another. But they had to keep moving. She swiftly entered a series of commands to seal off the auxiliary guard station. "Access to this station is shut off. But I can't disable those sentry droids from here." She could hear the hollow tone in her voice and it sickened her. "They are set in semi-autonomous mode."

Cindra was intensely looking at a diagram of some sort. "Come on, let's go," she barked with some urgency, and the two of them hurried forward, Cindra examining the pillars along the walls. "There it is." She brushed away a smudge of grime on the wall, revealing an old access panel to an unused maintenance transpod.

Reaching behind her back, she retrieved a small universal access key and placed it on the partially exposed section of the panel. A moment later there was a clicking sound, then the door slowly slid open.

"After you." Cindra extended her arm, motioning for Mirinda to precede her. After the door closed, the transpod slowly began to rise. It was clear it had not been used for a while.

"When the door opens, we need to get to cell numbers 161 and 185. After that we will go up one level." Cindra silently signaled with her weapon to wait as the door slid open. She threw a small recon sphere into the corridor. A live feed of the cellblock appeared in their visors. They could clearly see the cells ahead. "Good, no sentry droids. Let's go!"

They darted into the hallway, quickly finding the first cell. Using the same key device, Cindra placed it over the access panel. An energy burst erupted around the panel and the door opened after a few moments.

A humanoid male in standard detention clothing stood with his arms crossed in the center of the small cell. "Finally," he said with some irritation. "I am pleased to see you." He let his arms drift to the sides of his torso.

Not answering, Cindra threw a crystalline cube she plucked from her belt at him. He snatched it out of the air with a blinding speed that was unusual for his large size. With a practiced motion, he activated the smooth device. A holographic image of the compound, the escape route, as well as the time and extraction point hovered in the air in front of him.

"We have very little time. There is another large radiation cloud coming this way. It would be fatal if you were exposed to it," she said firmly.

"I've heard about that." He quirked an eyebrow at her and said somewhat cockily, "What about the others? I can assist you." He deactivated the device and placed it in his loose shirt pocket. It was clear to Mirinda that he and Cindra had some sort of personal connection.

"No, I have been given command of this mission. I order you to leave now. You will endanger the entire mission. Besides, I don't want to be held responsible for the death of one of our best operatives, okay?" she said huffily, but with an underlying determination.

He took in her unyielding expression. "Very well, Cindra," he said, quietly conceding to her authority. He looked Mirinda up and down, then nodded. Without another word, he left to find his way to safety.

"One more cell," Cindra said. When they reached it, she handed the key device to Mirinda. "Here, you repeat what I did and said."

Mirinda did as she ordered. A moment later, she was staring at a short, youthful human female with the face of a child. "What is this?" she muttered in disbelief. Aside from her childish appearance, the prisoner's air of grace and composure exposed her as the experienced agent she was.

"I guess they are recruiting from primary school these days. So young..." she said with dismay, unwittingly throwing the cube at the girl the same way Cindra had thrown the other cube at the first agent. The girl caught it effortlessly between her index finger and middle finger with machine-like precision.

"I am older than you think," said the girl. "The true measure of my value is in my capacity to solve puzzles that have answers that intertwine those of multidimensional equations. Ones that mere machines cannot answer, for they do not possess a soul, hence the catalyst to do so." The girl glanced at the holographic image display for a moment, then deactivated it and slid it into her vest pocket. "You are thinking of your friend Orisa. That is also a thing that machines can't do," she said with some pride, displaying something else entirely. The girl's eyes seemed ancient somehow. It was clear that there were spiritual gifts in her as well, dark ones at that.

Mirinda swallowed hard, then said with urgency, "Look, you must get going. Danger is heading this way, and it is not the android guards."

"It must have to do with the destruction of the Stadageo. Am I correct?" The stern look on her baby face seemed out of place. The young girl shot a glance at Cindra. "Happy to free your old boss?" Her remark was clearly aimed to irritate.

"Let's go," Cindra said through greeted teeth. She turned and strode away down the corridor without saying a word to the girl.

Mirinda caught up with her after a few quick steps. She looked briefly over her shoulder and was reassured to see the petite girl leaving the cellblock.

"Stop, a sentry droid is coming our way." Cindra's voice was fearless, just as she was. "It's time for a diversion." She folded her left arm across her chest and entered a series of codes on the metal surface of her wristband, signaling red team to cause a distraction.

Overcoming military sentry droids was not easy; just the thought set Mirinda's heart pounding in her chest. Feeling the tightness of her grip on the assault weapon, she hoped it would be powerful enough to save her life.

"We need to get to that transpod across the way to get to the next level up." Cindra's calm, steady voice went a long way to ease her fears. "All is clear now. The sentry has gone. Let's go." She strode with confidence across the short distance and entered the transpod. She placed the key she had used to open all the other doors on a raised bronze access panel just inside the cabin. Miranda breathed a sigh of relief, then braced herself to adjust to the gravity that was dragging at her body as they were whisked upward.

"Telfa Noor, I will need you to cover my left side. Prepare to fire immediately. Don't hesitate this time, if you want to survive." The way Cindra drawled it out made it clear she knew about Mirinda's earlier misgivings.

Mirinda pressed her lips together, nodding.

They took the time to check their weapons. As the transport slowed, they braced themselves on opposite sides of the doorway, just out of sight. The doors slid open to an eerie silence. It was clear that whatever diversion the red team had come up with had worked in drawing the sentry droids away. Mirinda let out a sigh of relief.

The lighting was brighter than expected, and they moved speedily in unison down the corridor. Suddenly, Cindra stopped at a wide section of a solid dark grey wall. "My reliable sources have informed me that this is a shielded entrance to a level one storage vault," she said low, looking for the minute clues that she had been given. "This is it. Put the key here." Cindra pointed to the partially hidden access panel.

Mirinda shakily placed the key on the faceplate next to Cindra's finger. The crackling sound of the force field deactivating was followed by an opening in the wall. Deactivating her shield visor, Mirinda stepped forward into the room beyond, and her heartbeat jolted.

Now, she understood the full ramifications of why she had been chosen to come on this mission.

"You need to identify only the most critical components needed for a Stadageo. Do it quickly," ordered Cindra.

Mirinda swallowed hard again, but did as ordered, walking up and down the rows of familiar devices and other internal components that had been taken from the Stadageo during regular repairs to sections of replication transformation pods. Cindra followed closely behind her, as if stalking prey.

I hope I can find some items that the Grand Dukar will be pleased with. Her spirit was repelled by the idea that they could be intending to create another ultimate super-agent. *No, I have to believe they'll use this advanced technology to be the dominant force in this sector of space...and that I can live with.*

"I will do my best, Cindra." Her flat tone disguised the discomfort roiling in her spirit. She pointed to several key auxiliary power relay regulators as they walked down the neatly organized rows. "These assist in controlling the amount of energy supplied to the necronos pods, which are partially constructed with materials from the realms of Creminmorta."

Feeling a dark, ugly sense about the room, Mirinda continued as swiftly as she could through each row, cataloging in detail the necessary parts. "Most of these items can be replicated. But I must warn you it will not be an easy task." She paused for a moment when she neared the end of the last row. Out of the corner of her eye, she noticed Cindra scanning every piece with a handheld device, then placing small pieces of computer systems into her pockets.

Just then, Mirinda caught sight of something that made her freeze. A data pad used by the Tisrak. Her skin began to crawl. That pad was used to input Nostrohelix equations that enabled the modifications in the necronos process. It sent a chill down her spine as she recalled her last encounter with the mysterious Stadageo taskmasters. It was a power that even the Overseers dared not cross. An image of the sprawled bodies of her mother and father appeared in her mind, accompanied by dark laughter and a voice saying, *"I got you."*

Mirinda shook her head to ward off the disturbing images.

"Looks like an ordinary data pad to me. How is it used?" Cindra picked it up and examined it, and casually handed it to Mirinda. "This damaged device contains enough data to create most of these items in this room."

Mirinda nodded, simultaneously disgusted and ecstatic she had found something the Grand Dukar would surely reward with a ship.

"Warning, high levels of radiation are imminent." The automated message echoed throughout the room.

"Take it and see if it can be repaired." Cindra activated her visor, as did Mirinda. "Good, we are done here, time to go catch our ride."

Relieved, Mirinda followed Cindra, who was already striding out of the room. Nausea hit her just then and she considered taking her last anti-radiation gel tablet. She dismissed the thought as quickly. "Not now…" she muttered under her breath.

"Not now, for what?" Cindra's question was sharp with concern. She was looking around to see if any danger was approaching.

"My gel tab. I think I am beginning to feel the effects of the radiation." Mirinda's chest began to ache with each step. She was glad they had reached the transpod. Cindra quickly closed the door after them.

"Eat your gel tab now, Telfa Norr," Cindra commanded as she propped her weapon against the wall. She deactivated her face shielding, popped a tab into her mouth, and quickly reactivated her protective headgear.

Mirinda did the same, leaning her head back on the wall momentarily. She could not seem to shake the strange visions of her deceased mother and father on Ramah. *Must be the effects of consuming too much Cymbratar.*

With stealth and speed, they headed to the extraction point. The cellblocks were deathly quiet. Mirinda thought about who might be in the cells they were passing.

"Telfa Norr, we can't help them." Cindra's blunt statement was firm. "Keep going or we will share their fate and die of radiation poisoning."

Mirinda's head jerked in surprise; it was as if Cindra could read her mind. Just like the little girl did earlier.

Before she could speak, a powerful and violent explosion rocked them and knocked them to their knees. Mirinda gasped and threw an arm over her head instinctively. Chunks of rubble fell as the ceiling collapsed ahead of them, blocking their path.

"Well, it looks as though we will have to find another way out of here," said Cindra tersely.

They ran back down the cellblock toward the main detention intersection. Entering a junction that connected to a secondary security complex, they kept moving with weapons drawn. Without any choice, they headed out into the open. Dread filled Mirinda's gut as she spotted sentry droids approaching in their direction.

"Run to that lift, now!" Cindra yelled. Without a word, Mirinda matched her stride for stride.

"We have company," Mirinda said between gasps of air. Her eyes darted to Cindra, making sure she was protecting her flank. Cindra swiftly lifted her assault weapon and fired a volley of blasts in short succession into the nearest sentry droid. It was clear she was an expert marksman, as the precisely aimed shots hit the metal guard at critical locations, causing it to explode. Streaks of yellow energy blazed past her shoulder from the other sentry droids returning fire.

"Come on! Get on this lift platform." Cindra's voice was filled with sharp urgency.

Mirinda winced as her body armor was pelted with multiple hits from the droids, jarring her whole body. At a dead run, she dove onto the lift belly-down, almost knocking Cindra over. She quickly rolled up onto one knee, ready to fire. From her vantage point she saw five sentry droids changing configuration. The bottom of their torsos glowed with power as they prepared to rocket into the air and follow them.

"We have sentry droids coming up from below," Cindra yelled.

"I see them!" Mirinda shot to her feet and began firing rapidly at them, to no effect.

"Target their propulsion control systems, near the bottom section," Cindra commanded as she fired her weapon at the droid farthest to the right.

Mirinda ducked just in time, avoiding an incoming energy blast. Her visor displayed and highlighted the target area. With measured bursts of energy, she hit the sentry droid's flight system, sending it crashing into a nearby wall. The explosion buffeted their bodies for a second. A blast struck her left shoulder, rocking her upper body backward for a moment. She grimaced at the extreme heat that accompanied the hit. Adrenaline coursed through her, accompanied by an unfamiliar rage.

Time seemed to still, and as if in slow motion she saw a single blast hit Cindra's chest, lifting her off her feet and slamming her into the back wall of the partially enclosed lift. She heard the metallic scrape of body armor a heartbeat later. *No!* thought Mirinda.

Laser-focused now, Mirinda allowed all of her anger to stream down through her arm, as if it were giving the weapon more power. Her concentrated fire took out another sentry, which then careened into two others. They dropped like dead weights. Even with her heightened senses, she was not able to destroy the fifth sentry droid, who was gaining on them.

"Hold on. Brace yourself, we are going to make an emergency stop in three...two...one." Cindra's strained voice held pain.

Mirinda squatted down as best she could, bracing her left arm beneath the rail, all the while discharging her weapon at the approaching droid. The platform shuddered as it screeched to a halt. She let go of the railing and tried to hit the droid. Too late, its energy blasts struck her weapon, shattering it.

Cindra, who seemed to have recovered, returned fire and finally destroyed the sentry. The dull red and yellow glow on the railing from the combined firepower of the sentry droids was a reminder that they had barely escaped with their lives. Mirinda regained her balance and took a deep breath, joining Cindra, who immediately shot the control panel with her handheld weapon.

"That will hold them off for a while," Cindra said triumphantly. "Come on, this way to the auxiliary landing platform." She paused to reload her weapon. "There should be no sentries there. But if there are, our transport ship will dispatch them easily enough." Cindra let out a faint growl of pain as they began to move. Mirinda knew by her hunched walk with a slight stagger that she was more than slightly injured.

As if she could discern Mirinda's desperate desire to help her, Cindra turned and said sharply, "We are a little early, but be ready to run to the ship when I say so, got it?" The access key device easily broke through the security code and the heavy door slowly opened. Cindra's weapon was pointed at the empty landing platform.

Great, no security droids! Mirinda's excitement was quickly dampened as she remembered the radiation levels were rising quickly. *If the ship doesn't come soon, I'll die, and this mission will be a failure making Orisa's chances of escaping off world slim at best.* Fear rose as she remembered Orisa's hopeless tone. *Be careful.*

Like hope rising after a storm, a small bulky ship emerged from beneath the edge of the sea cliffs. Without a moment's pause, they ran to the open side door in the hull. With the ship still moving, they dove into the opening. Mirinda landed hard on her left shoulder, the one that had sustained the hit earlier on the lift. "Aaaahhh." She panted, bracing against the pain, and rolled over onto her back.

Remaining still, she took stock of her condition and felt the slight jostling of the ship as it sped away. She picked up her aching left arm with her right hand and read the radiation levels on her armored sleeve. "Only one red bar, good, we are safe," she said with a gusty sigh. She deactivated her face shield, gritting her teeth. As she breathed the cold, moldy, acidic air of the cargo bay, the nausea that had left threatened to return.

Cindra was putting the two Stadageo components she had been carrying back into a large container. She turned, extending her hand. "Give me the data pad," she ordered, then lifted a highly polished flask to her lips and drank deeply.

Mirinda stood up slowly and tossed the data pad to Cindra, who cupped its weight with her free hand in midair and let gravity direct the pad into the container. It clattered lightly against the other components.

"Here, drink this. It will repair any damage the Cremindraux radiation has done to your body and speed the healing of the injury to your shoulder." Her tone was mild and her face held a lightly veiled curiosity. She capped the bottle and tossed it to Mirinda. "It's not as refined and effective as Cymbratar, but it will do the job."

She is testing me. Mirinda let the flask hit her chest, catching it while still looking at Cindra's weary face with a cocked eyebrow. She opened the chromed flask. The stench of it hit her nostrils and made her eyes water. But she bravely lifted it and drank a large gulp. She immediately began gagging, but determined to pass the newbie test, shot down a second large swallow of the smelly substance. Afterward, she closed the flask back up and tossed it back to Cindra.

"Believe or not, I've tasted worse," she said, as if she had done it many times before. She bent over slightly, bracing her arms on her knees, and felt the welcome relief that was flooding her battered and bruised body. The healing, rejuvenating effects were coursing through her veins.

"It helps the healing process by using the Cymbratar that is already in your body." Cindra grinned at her as she began to remove her body armor.

"I assume I should do the same?" Mirinda removed her headgear and moved closer to the senior Choshek agent.

"Yep, drop it all in here." Cindra tossed her armor into a container marked with a radiation symbol. She moved to the other side of the cargo bay and opened a cabinet.

Mirinda stripped off her battered and charred body armor and reflected on how close she had come to dying this time.

"Here, wear this." Mirinda turned just in time to catch her new uniform. She lifted the nano fiber flex bodysuit up to herself to gauge the fit. She could only hope that it would complement her own less athletic frame as well as it did Cindra's lean lanky frame. She pulled it on, admiring how good she looked in the figure-flattering suit.

"Before we meet Dukar Suun in Nodramesh, we will have to change ships in the town of Yanshun."

Cindra's remark sparked a horrific thought. "Wait…where is the rest of our team?"

A bark of sarcastic laughter mocked Mirinda's concern. "Actually, we missed the first extraction ship. They are all accounted for. Fortunately for us, Dukar Suun wanted to make sure he got the Stadageo components so badly that he set up this second extraction point as a contingency," Cindra said as she started moving in short bursts of Kohyim-like motions to re-strengthen her body and mind.

Mirinda followed suit, relief flooding her body as the well-loved rejuvenation exercises from her youth gave her a measure of peace.

A bright light flashed in the cargo hold, followed by a humanoid-sounding voice announcing, "We are now landing in Yanshun, prepare to disembark immediately."

"Dukar Suun sounds like a wonderful individual," Mirinda said sarcastically, finishing the last fluid motion of the routine.

"You can thank him yourself in person, shortly," Cindra said in an obtuse tone. Standing next to the door, she said mildly, "Come on."

Mirinda stepped out of the transport, heading straight to their waiting ship across the way.

Mirinda sensed the strong oppressive presence of clandestine operatives that filled the atmosphere. Looking out of the private transport viewport, she watched vast numbers of Varkrato League and Tartarus government workers building massive multiphasic barriers just south of the Omsook mountain ranges, in the effort to protect the hundred million citizens of Magiathep from the threat of Cremindraux radiation in the distance.

"Do you think the barriers will hold the radiation back?" She blurted out the question as she grappled with the realization that she could be responsible for the destruction of the entire capital city of Necropis.

"Don't worry, there are many Krauvanok engineers assigned to oversee the project. The strange Tisrak beings who have provided the necessary power generators, the likes we have never seen before, are also there working alongside them." Cindra's confidence bordered on arrogance. "So, yes, I believe the barrier will hold back the radiation. Do you have family on Magiathep?"

"No." She kept her voice deliberately light, but dread filled her heart at the possibility that she might encounter the Tisrak.

"Prepare to disembark." The pilot's voice was mature, indicating he was well seasoned.

It seemed like an eternity since she'd last seen Orisa, now her only true family, if truth be told. *My loyal friend and beloved sister in spirit.*

She felt the ship decelerate and turn. Out of the viewport she watched other ships landing in the hub. Her thoughts turned to her beloved home world of Ramah, which she hoped she would soon be returning to—so long as the Dukar kept his promise—and her heart beat faster in excitement.

"Landing sequence initiated. Prepare to disembark once the bay doors are opened." The announcement was a pleasant sound to her ears. As the ship landed, she rose to her feet and adjusted her clothing. Her eyes met Cindra's impassive look.

"Let's go, shall we?" Cindra said, smiling. *The time when I don't have to follow you will not come soon enough.* "What did you say?" Cindra turned and cocked her head to the side.

"I didn't say anything. I am just following you as instructed." Mirinda kept her expression impassive. She would have to guard herself carefully with this one.

An unknown path lay ahead, filled with uncertainty.

Chapter Nine

LETALIS

"Maybe this was a bad idea after all." Taona was frustrated that her commandeered transport was unable to maintain power to the engines any longer. She decided it was much better to execute a controlled descent than to crash-land. *Well, I almost made it all the way there,* she thought with a sigh. She decreased her speed and skimmed twenty meters over the jungle canopy. *Good, I believe that will do.*

Her thought was intruded upon by the ship's automated alarm. "Status of power core levels at critical, failure imminent."

With a sigh, she guided the transport toward a small clearing. "Doesn't seem too far away from my destination." The ancient path was covered by deep jungle vegetation, but seemed passable. *At least it leads straight to the stone temple. Of course it had to be an abandoned site in the middle of nowhere.* She was upset with herself for strictly following instructions not to bring any weapon. *I can slip on my utility belt.* She looked at the fragmentation spheres it contained, hesitating. "No, I better not." Obeying the demands of the religious order who'd called her here seemed important.

Her body tensed tightly when the control panel went dark. A moment later she was jostled violently as the ship smashed to the ground. She remained motionless for a moment, then relaxed, seeing that her cargo was firmly secure in the adjacent pilot seat. She gingerly touched her bottom lip with a gloved hand. "I hope biting my lip is the worst that will happen on this trek." Her pessimistic tone snapped her out of her impending self-pity.

After releasing her seatbelt, she stood up and peered out of the transparent canopy, on the lookout for opportunistic predators searching for their next meal. "I can't stay here, even with this protective clothing it would not be wise." She removed the small ornate box and the beautifully crafted gold shoulder broaches inlayed with precious jewels, and left the smoking vessel.

With sheer determination, she made her way through thick patches of hanging vines until she reached the old path she had seen from above. *The old temple looks to be slightly more than two kilometers away.* "Not exactly wearing the best attire for traveling on foot in the humid climate of the Tonguton jungle." She grumbled as she wiped the sweat from her forehead with the transparent veil of the hood of the strange clothing she wore. *At least these items are not too burdensome to carry.* Adjusting her grip on the ornate box and the jewel-encrusted broaches of the high-ranking deceased priestess, Taona concentrated on her footing between the dense branches that crisscrossed the pathway.

She really wished she'd just worn her utility belt. Every snap and rustle in the jungle made her certain something was about to jump out and attack her.

Still on high alert, a few steps later Taona came upon a small hairy predator that was obviously dead. *One less animal to be concerned about.* A few moments later, more carcasses of the little beasts appeared in her path. "Must be a family... It's the radiation." She was aware of the gloom and burgeoning despair in her hushed tone. She halted her dark thoughts and continued with increased haste toward the temple. "Almost there."

Taona paused as she suddenly entered a clearing. "I knew it...a religious site," she said smugly, then her grin vanished. *I can almost sense the spirits of the long departed. Most likely those who were sacrificed. I hope I don't join them.*

Her dark musings were broken by the appearance of an individual a hundred meters ahead, standing in an archway. A human female. As Taona got closer, she could see the woman's body was completely enveloped in a fine, dark mist. Her clothes were similar to those worn by the High Priestess from the earlier encounter. *Must be a lower-ranking member*, Taona thought, noticing the woman's shoulder broaches were smaller in size and much less intricate.

The crunch of dried leaves accompanied her ascent on the stairs. *I like their style. They certainly know how to dress to impress...beautifully designed clothes.* The woman was short and her white hair was intricately laced with gold chains. Her large, deep blue eyes seemed unnatural. *She must have consumed Cymbratar for quite some time.* Taona patted her forehead with her veil and then came to a stop directly in front of her.

"Good, you wore the clothes I sent you." The priestess' calm tone exuded confidence that added to her stature. She glanced at the items Taona was cradling in her arms. "Follow me, I must prepare for the arrival of the High Priestess." She turned away and vanished through the vegetative veil. Taona stared at the dead birds and other creatures that dotted the walks of the stone temple as she followed, and grimaced.

"You stand over there. Leave your hood on. Do not remove it!" the priestess commanded. Her stern countenance insinuated dire consequences if Taona didn't obey.

She stood silently and observed with fascination as the priestess extended her hands toward a thick obelisk. Blue tendrils of energy discharged from her hands, energizing the bronze monolith. Taona hoped this wouldn't take too long, as she was already anxious to leave this place.

Just moments before, Nia had dropped off the recovered items to Dukar Gruppa. She then excused herself, claiming another duty, and promised to return shortly to claim their ship. She was well aware that blood sacrifices of living souls was common practice in Kravjin spawned religions. A vivid image of a regal woman dressed in religious robes rose in front of her eyes. The ceremonial blade that she held was dripping with blood. She knew she was right to follow Taona as this confirmed her suspicions.

"Taona, you are in great danger. I need to be there as back-up just in case." Nia muttered to herself, and diverted more power to the sensor array to compensate for the radiation interference. She maneuvered the Class II swift antigravity glider between a mountain and a valley, then down the mountainside toward a lush green jungle. "What are you doing that you had to travel to the middle of nowhere to do it?" She shook her head, deeply puzzled.

"Warning, high levels of Thamak radiation detected," sounded the ship computer.

"Death by Thamak or Cremindraux radiation...lovely." Her sarcastic tone did little to lift her spirits. She noted the location beacon displayed on the control panel. Taona didn't know that she had placed a tracking device on her utility belt when they parted ways earlier. *She will be so mad at me for following her. Not too far now.* The panel flickered. *Oh well, friends don't abandon friends. Besides, I just want to make sure she is not in any danger.* She vaguely noted one of the Letalis moons rising over the sea of towering trees. A sense of urgency drove her to go even faster. *I have to get to Taona.*

The location beacon indicated the transmitter was some thirty kilometers distant. Since it was not moving, she knew that for whatever reason, Taona was not wearing the belt or had reached her destination.

"What is that?" She frowned at the top of a stone structure in the distance. "Great, she has to be in there somewhere," she said triumphantly, finally reaching a clearing big enough to land. *That's a path of some kind to that structure. I'd better land behind it and out of sight.* She maneuvered the glider very close behind what she now recognized as a pyramid. "This is a little tight, but it will have do," she remarked as she slowly set the ship down between the intertwined branches.

She quickly powered down the glider, adjusted her headgear, then activated her visor and surveyed the surroundings, searching for danger. The radiation indicator on the left side of her visor was blinking strongly, warning of the danger just outside the sleek transport. "Of course you went to a place affected by the destroyed Stadageo." Her tone was filled with quiet derision. "If only I had more Cymbratar..." Her voice trailed off in irritation. *It's now or never.*

She inspected her TK74 short-barreled weapon once more and holstered it. Quickly, she counted three Class IV Close Proximately Devastators (CPDs) on either side of her utility belt. *Who knows what trouble awaits me when I reach Taona.* She pulled the Audraba long blade out of the scabbard at her side, and her head dipped as she swallowed hard. "Moshiach be with me."

Nia plunged ahead with careful grace, in an effort to not trip over fallen branches as she ducked under and vaulted over them. She would have to be extra careful in her recon of the area before she went in. A trail of rain slithered down her visor as she peered through the dripping shrubs in front of her. *Only a hundred meters, now. But wait, what is that?* She pulled back, then moved fifty meters to the right to get a better view. The decayed ruins of a city lay just ahead, but a strange snapping noise from above caught her attention.

With blinding speed, she had her weapon in hand, ready to defend herself. A half dozen yellow and red birds crashed to the ground around her, and she nearly shrieked aloud, covering her head and jumping to avoid them. *Thamak, with traces of Cremindraux radiation.* Her visor flickered with the information. Her stomach clenched in dread that the same fate might befall her.

Something told her she should not go through the main entrance.

Maybe I can find a side entrance. Shoving her misgivings aside, she took one last look at the sprawled birds, then slid the Audraba long blade out once again. In a methodical way, she cut the dense vines that covered a trail to the side of the pyramid.

This looks like an entrance. The creeping jungle growth had long since overtaken the door to the building. With her trusty weapon palmed, Nia cautiously slipped through a partially open gate. Even with her enhanced sensory visor, the place was dim. She imagined it smelled of rot. *I better go this way.* She chose to go up a narrow ramp.

Suddenly Nia's visor picked up the sound of someone speaking. She stopped behind a stone pillar, retracted the visor to hear better, then reactivated it. *That's a woman's voice, but it does not sound like Taona.* She silently stepped off the ramp and stealthily moved toward a nearby balcony. Above the chamber were glimmering gemstones adorning a ten-meter-wide oculus. A moving shadow out of the corner of her eye flitted over the oculus and stopped as if it saw her, then dove quickly out of sight.

"It is time." Nia's spirit was troubled to hear the strange woman's authoritative voice echo loudly in the chamber.

She felt compelled to see what was going on below, and removed a small section of her visor that acted as a mirror and placed it on top of the balcony. *Who is that woman standing next to Taona? It looks like she is wearing some kind of religious clothing.* They were standing directly in front of two thick obelisks that were engraved with cursive hieroglyphs, with a single reptilian eye at the top of each. A single metal band arced vertically over the four-meter span between the monoliths. Nia vaguely noted with relief that the radiation levels were lower in here. *Must be the result of the kind of stone used here... Who knows for sure.* Her thoughts trailed off as she noted with curiosity a small ornate chest cradled in the crook of Taona's left elbow. Even from this distance she could see the single blue gem sparkling on the top. *Is that the reason you had to come alone?* "I wonder what's inside," she whispered.

As she watched, the obelisks began to glow, and the band split into two sections. A large translucent sphere formed in between the two pieces. In its center was a black ball from which emerged a hauntingly beautiful human woman clothed in regal blue vestments.

"I am High Priestess of the Order of Aggrevox." Her authoritative, mature tone of voice made it clear she wielded a great deal of power and influence. Taona and the other woman bowed in respect.

"Greetings, my High Priestess," said the shorter woman at Taona's side. Nia saw a shadow swirling around the High Priestess, then it vanished into one of the glowing obelisks.

"Did you remove all evidence of work from the laboratory where you found this sacred box?" Nia could see the glare of her large blue eyes even from this distance.

"Yes, I did as I was instructed," said Taona, with confidence. "Every log entry regarding what was done in that necronos laboratory has been deleted. I also made sure the computer cores were completely destroyed. No trace of evidence remains."

"Good... Now give Sister Nadezda the chest and the items removed from Priestess Tmexa's garments." The voice of the High Priestess was laced with dark undertones that had an acidic bite to them. Taona did as she said, handing the objects to the woman at her side.

"Nadezda, stand behind me." The priestess' nostrils flared in her brightly glowing face with distaste as if she were looking at an insect.

Taona stood poised and calm, waiting until the other woman stepped behind the High Priestess. "I kept my end of the bargain. Now are you going to keep yours?" Her voice was firm, but a thread of uncertainty laced the brusque question.

"The agreement was for you to come alone. You were told several times to do so. Need I remind you I said if you failed there would be dire consequences?" The icy cold threat was clear even from where Nia crouched silently. Sibilant whispers echoed in the chamber and a dark shadowy presence loomed over them.

"What are you referring to?" retorted Taona. "I came alone as requested." Her hands flung out with great surprise and a slight challenge.

Nia felt sick to her stomach as she became aware of the recon drone hovering silently behind her. She had been so caught up in the events unfolding below that it caught her off guard. She looked at it and the palm-size drone quickly darted out of sight. Turning back to the mirror, she noted that Taona was looking at the upper floors for the intruder.

"You brought someone along. They are on the third level... This is not acceptable!" The High Priestess thundered, enraged. A terrible scowl horribly distorted her formerly beautiful face. It appeared that something else inhabited her that was just now showing itself. She flung out her arms toward Taona. "Mekka Tommu Salom!" she shouted.

Taona's garments dissolved, leaving her clad only in her form-fitting flex suit. The woman at the High Priestess' side gave Taona a scowling stare, curled her lip, and followed her spiritual leader back through the translucent portal that snapped shut behind them. Nia stood up and leaned over the railing to find Taona glaring at her with disbelief.

"What in Creminmorta are you doing here?" Taona's voice matched the rage the High Priestess had just released into the room. Nia dashed down a ramp, running to the first floor.

"I told you not to follow me." There was some relief in Taona's voice, as she seemed to be more herself now, but she was still talking frantically. "I am not sure what the dire consequences are but I am sure they won't be pleasant." She shook her head at Nia, watching her scan the area with her weapon drawn.

"We can't use my ship, the power cores are damaged beyond repair," Taona stated flatly.

"Let's use the glider I borrowed, it has more than enough room for the both of us and it's only a few hundred meters from here." Nia looked at Taona's shivering frame and said quietly, "You won't last long without protective gear. Let's go… This way." She turned and led the way out.

Nia glanced behind her and noticed Taona clutching her chest.

She had a look of intense pain on her face, and coughed loudly with an ugly hitch as they reached the glider. Nia gripped her friend by the upper arm and assisted her into the small transport.

"This looks uncomfortable," Taona whined, gasping for her next breath. "These seats are for children." She covered her mouth as she was seized with an even longer reverberating cough, plopping herself in the adjoining seat. She cradled her head on her arms that were resting on her bent knees.

"Sit tight, Taona, we are going to get you some help." Nia tossed her weapon down and flipped the control panel switch on.

It lit up momentarily, then went offline.

What's happening? Nia's heart was pounding. "Give me a second, I need to check something out." She could barely hold back the tears as she realized the glider's power cells had been removed. "Who did this...?"

Without the power cells, the glider wouldn't fly. They couldn't leave this place.

A wordless shout burst out of her, and she slammed her fist on the panel that bounced back and nearly hit her in the face. She refused to give up, but it was too much all of a sudden. A dull ache was forming in her temples. "Maybe we can find a safe place in the temple." Her words were void of conviction. "Come on, Taona, let's go back there."

She helped Taona back out of the glider. Taona took several steps before she collapsed to the ground. Even Nia's hands could not get her back up.

"I am not going to make it, my friend." Taona's voice was reedy thin with agony and grief. She dragged herself backwards with Nia's help to lean against a tree.

Nia shook her head back and forth violently, but could not stop the flood of tears that began to stream down her face. She knelt at Taona's side, looking into her graying face. "Why did you come alone?" She had to know the truth. Her eyes followed a stream of blood trickling from Taona's nose.

Taona nodded, weakly acquiescing. "You heard the woman say I was told to come alone. But there is more…" She coughed sharply into her hand, and Nia could see blood glistening in her quickly hidden palm. "Listen, while you were on the floor unconscious back in that laboratory, that priestess appeared. She requested that I deliver the items I took off of the dead priestess from the chamber. Remember that female, Etrakkian?" Nia nodded, swallowing hard, trying to contain her grief. "They were hers. I was also asked to deliver an ornate chest. I believe it contained a finished portion of the new Nembratar… Well, that's my guess anyway. I didn't check." She coughed even more violently into her hand again spitting up more blood. "In exchange we would be taken to any place I desired… Nia, I wanted us to go home." Her weak tone was pitiful, but she looked into Nia's eyes with love and mercy.

Nia gently wiped off a trickle of blood that was coming out of Taona's nose, trying to figure out what to say. She removed her protective headgear and flung it forcefully away. "Please, please forgive me, my friend." She collapsed onto Taona's lap and began to cry with great remorse.

Taona gently placed her hand on Nia's head. "Don't worry. I love you, and I forgive you. Now go get that helmet and save yourself…" Her words were growing more and more labored.

But Nia shook her head. She sat up and took off all her protective clothing, placing it over Taona, who was too weak to protest. She kissed her forehead. "No," she said in a hushed tone.

It all came out of her in a helpless rush. The words blended quickly together as she sought to help Taona understand why she'd followed her. "I delivered the box to Dukar Gruppa as you asked. Then, I tracked you because I thought I could help you if you were in danger. I should have listened to you, now look what I did to you, I am so sorry." Her voice was loud in her travail as tears streaked down her cheeks.

She began to sob uncontrollably at the devastation unfolding in front of her. "Please, please forgive me my friend, we have lost everything, so much death and sorrow." She collapsed onto Taona's lap once more.

"All is forgiven…now please go and save yourself." Taona's words were a mere whisper now.

A cloud of warmth seemed to surround them and the tears ebbed. She was aware of a golden glow that was enveloping Taona, and kissed her on the forehead one final time, knowing what was coming. "Stop asking me to leave you, I won't do it, you won't be alone," she said in a soft, tear-blurred voice, and wiped the stream of blood from her own nose with her sleeve.

Nia coughed, then cleared her throat and began to sing softly the well-remembered song they had learned as children. "Hand in hand, we walk on the path lit by HIS glory, Let us sing praises to HIS majesty. Let us rejoice. Let us rejoice... Hand in hand, HIS love sustains us and by His grace eternal life. Hand in hand, let us sing HIS praises forevermore."

Taona whispered the last words with her, then closed her eyes and stopped breathing. Nia removed her gloves and held tightly onto Taona's limp hands.

"Hand in hand..." She coughed hard and spit out blood, then continued to sing. Her own breathing was starting to feel shallow. A low groan issued from her throat with a rattling cough. Her head felt as though it would explode. Death was very close now. She held on tightly to Taona's hand for as long as she could, sensing her own organs failing.

"Hand in hand..." Her soft voice lilted one more time. She turned her head and slumped to the ground. The curtain of her life shut, and death arrived.

Yaqal 21

The last petal of the flower of my life says glory to Abba El and HIS Messiah. May the song of my heart reach HIS courts and be pleasing to the creator of my soul as I pass into eternity.

A single individual wearing a radiation suit stood over the outstretched sisters. The area surrounding them was strangely peaceful and it felt almost sacred. One of them was lying with an arm outstretched, with her hand open as if she had been reaching for something just out of sight. He crouched down and looked into their faces curiously. He had seen many go before, but they never looked like this. "What were you two doing here in the middle of the jungle? Were you making sacrifices in that temple?" the Muak'Xod agent said in puzzlement.

Dukar Gruppa stepped into his private quarters and decoded a priority one message:

Dukar Gruppa, I have located the glider and agents Nia and Taona as ordered. Data scan readings indicate death by Thamak and Cremindraux radiation. Waiting for further instructions.

He recalled that these two were actually rogue sisters that were worth quite a large bounty. *How can I profit from this? Oh, I know, I will preserve them and use them as leverage somehow. Grand Dukar Bharata will be pleased, collecting a large bounty tax for two lifeless bodies. He laughed. I am so clever. So those are rogues sisters. Interesting, they don't seem dangerous to me. I wonder if they had anything to do with the destruction of the Stadageo? No matter, this will elevate my standing above that treacherous Gwauth.* He bared his sharp, stained teeth.

"Gwauth, you are no match for me. I will be the one ascending to the seat of Grand Dukar, leader of the Muak'Xod," he said aloud. He paused for a moment. "Where is Raduu?" Without second-guessing himself, he entered the new instructions.

Place them in stasis units, then bring them to Chevkasoon station in Tepha. End of transmission.

Now I have to contact Raduu to collect the bodies, he thought, a smirk spreading across his face. *Things are finally going my way.*

MARIUM KAHNET OATH

Every member of the Marium Kahnet sisterhood must take the sacred oath and those who wish to live their lives accordingly are also encouraged to take the oath.

THE SHABAUH

I pledge my life as a vessel of light as I step through the veil of divine purpose. I am cleansed in purity. My head is adorned with humility. The ways of the Marium Kahnet are my life, my heart, and my soul belongs to Abba El and in HIS messiah is my salvation.

Marium Kahnet Book Trilogy

RETRIBUTION Available

DECIMATION Available

REBIRTH Available

SOCIAL MEDIA LINKS

www.mariumkahent.com

www.facebook.com/mariumkahnet

83244299R00109

Made in the USA
Columbia, SC
23 December 2017